HER AMISH WISH

BOOK 37 THE AMISH BONNET SISTERS

SAMANTHA PRICE

CHAPTER 1

*W*ilma opened her eyes as the first rays of dawn stretched across the sky. But before she could fully wake, the phone's shrill ring in the barn pierced the air.

With a surge of adrenaline, she dashed down the stairs to the backdoor, hastily slipping into her boots, propelled by a sense of urgency. Who could be calling at this early hour?

It could only mean one thing. Someone was in trouble. Thoughts of her distant daughters and faraway grandchildren raced through her mind, casting shadows of worry.

As Wilma's trembling hand was about to grasp the receiver, the ring abruptly ceased, leaving her huffing in exasperation.

The phone rang again, and she seized the receiver

with determination, her voice echoing her worry. "Hello? Who is it? What's happened?"

"Everything's fine. It's me, Earl."

Wilma could sense the bubbling excitement in Earl's voice, and she knew exactly what it meant. "Have you...?"

"We have two perfectly healthy boys."

She closed her eyes, silently saying a prayer of thanks. "Boys? I'm overjoyed for you. Did everything go well? How is Miriam?"

"She's fine. Everyone's doing great."

Wilma exhaled a breath she didn't realize she had been holding. "Good." The relationship with her eldest stepson had always been strained. She had been impatient with him, struggling to adjust to the sudden role of a mother and the weight of an instant family. "I'm happy for both of you."

"Thanks, Wilma. It was touch and go at the beginning, but the doctors did an outstanding job. Miriam is resting now, and I'm right outside the ward, marveling at my two beautiful boys."

Wilma's heart swelled at the mere thought of cradling those precious babies in her arms. "Maybe you could use my help? I could lend an extra pair of hands around the house."

There was a pause at the other end of the line, and Wilma could almost picture Earl's hesitant expression.

"No, it's fine, Wilma. We've got all the help we need for now."

A pang of regret hit Wilma. She remembered the harsh words she had said to Earl when he had announced his engagement to Miriam, a woman much older than him. "Oh, I see." Miriam had defied her expectations. Despite Miriam's age, she had given birth to two sets of twins and even a set of triplets. "I can visit, though, *jah?*"

Again, a pause. "I'll bring them to you. We'll all visit as soon as we're able."

"I'd love that. I truly would. I know it might be challenging to travel with children, but I want to see them while they're still little."

"I must go now. Miriam needs me."

"Of course, Earl. Please give her my love. And take care of yourself, too," Wilma said with genuine concern.

"I will. Bye."

As Wilma hung up the phone's receiver, relief washed over her. Everything had turned out fine for Earl and Miriam, and that was a comfort. Yet, a tinge of sadness clung to her heart, refusing to let go.

As she walked back to the house, her steps were heavy, each one echoing with unspoken apologies and the rhythm of 'what ifs.'

If only they lived closer, she thought. It would be so much easier to mend the wounds of the past, to show Earl how deeply she loved him and that she had always cared. That's what his father would have wanted.

But deep down, Wilma wondered if it was too late

to turn back the hands of time. Were some mistakes irreversible?

Nevertheless, as she stepped through the door, she held onto a glimmer of hope. Maybe, just maybe, there would still be moments in the future to prove her love, to heal the wounds, and to create new memories.

As Wilma stepped into the kitchen, she glanced at the clock to see it was only five in the morning. A tired sigh escaped her lips, and she retreated to her bed, hoping to steal a few more moments of rest before the day moved on.

An hour later, the morning sun filtered through the curtains, casting a warm glow in the room. Weariness still clung to her bones, but she knew it was time to embrace the day. The sounds of morning activity from the kitchen below nudged her from her sleep.

Wilma drew back the curtains, inviting in the light. She dressed in one of her better dresses, meticulously arranged her hair, and carefully placed her prayer *kapp* upon her head. Today, she would joyfully announce the arrival of Miriam and Earl's twins.

On entering the kitchen, Wilma discovered Debbie already seated at the table, eating alongside Krystal and Jared.

"Good morning, everyone," Wilma greeted them, settling into a chair.

Debbie glanced up, acknowledging her presence. "Morning, Wilma."

"I've prepared breakfast," Krystal announced, her voice brimming with pride.

"Denke." Wilma looked at the array of scrambled eggs, toast, bacon, waffles, and hashbrowns arranged in the center of the table. Jared loved his hashbrowns, and Debbie and Krystal often made them for him. "I must have overslept."

"It'll do you good. You probably needed the extra sleep," Debbie remarked, spreading a generous layer of butter on her toast.

Krystal had a better look at Wilma. "Aren't you going to eat?"

Wilma paused, her gaze shifting from Krystal to the spread before her. With a soft smile, she reached for a plate and set it in front of her. "I will in a minute."

"Oh, good. I'll get you some coffee."

"Denke." Wilma couldn't help but notice the wide grin on Krystal's face, which hinted at the arrival of Jed. He was expected for breakfast along with Ada and Samuel. "It all looks lovely. I might save my appetite to eat with Ada. I'm too excited at the moment."

Debbie looked over at Wilma. "Why the excitement?"

Wilma's eyes sparkled as she waited for Krystal to sit down. "I received a call early this morning. Earl and Miriam's twins have arrived. They're here, and they're doing well."

A squeal of delight escaped from Krystal, her radiant smile reflecting Wilma's joy.

Debbie's brows knitted together in concern. "And Miriam? Is she alright?"

Wilma nodded, a warm glow of contentment spreading through her. "Yes, Miriam and the boys are all in good health. I didn't think to ask for their names."

"Congratulations on becoming a grandmother again, Wilma," Debbie said, her voice soft yet sincere.

Wilma beamed. *"Denke."*

A knock at the door interrupted their conversation. Wilma rose from her seat. "That must be Samuel and Ada. Come in!" As she neared the front door, a moment of realization froze her in place—Ada never knocked. The knock could only mean it was someone else.

Just then, the door opened and Obadiah poked his head through the doorway. "Hello."

Wilma's heart skipped a beat as their eyes met.

CHAPTER 2

"Good morning, Wilma," Obadiah said, smiling.

"Good morning."

"I've come to lend Samuel a hand in fixing the porch railing. We thought we'd make an early start."

"Thank you. That's very kind of you." At that moment, as their gazes intertwined, Wilma couldn't help but be grateful for the familiar face in her life. It seemed God was weaving intricate threads, intertwining their lives once more. It was then that Wilma noticed Jed had been standing behind Obadiah.

"We're not too early, I hope," Jed voiced his concern from the doorway.

Before she could respond, Obadiah said, "Are you aware there's someone asleep on your porch, Wilma?"

Wilma wasn't sure if she'd heard him correctly. "What was that?"

Obadiah swung the door open wide, silently beckoning her to look outside. Stepping through the doorway, Wilma saw Samuel and Ada standing over a body on her porch. Squinting, she soon recognized the person—it was Matthew, wrapped in a sleeping bag.

Ada wore a distressed expression, her mouth pressed into a thin line, and her cheeks appeared sunken. She always felt responsible for Matthew's actions, given he was her nephew.

With a cough meant to rouse him, Ada attempted to wake Matthew, but there was no response. She coughed again, this time louder, but was still met with silence.

"It's no use. He has always been able to sleep through anything." Samuel mirrored Ada's discontent. Leaning down, Samuel held his hand in front of Matthew's nose. "At least he's still breathing."

Jed moved forward to join everyone as they gathered around Matthew. "What's going on with him?"

"Probably something to do with Krystal, I would imagine. Let's leave him here for now and head inside where it's warmer," Ada suggested, her face filled with embarrassment as she walked past Wilma toward the front door.

Jed couldn't help but find amusement in the situation. He stole one last glance at Matthew, peacefully snoozing before following everyone inside. Krystal welcomed Jed with excitement, but her enthusiasm quickly waned as she noticed the peculiar behavior of Wilma and Ada.

"What's wrong?" Krystal inquired.

"Matthew is asleep on the porch." Ada passed by Krystal and took a seat at the kitchen table.

"What?" Krystal turned to Jed, who wore an entertained smirk.

"Why don't you go take a look for yourself," he replied.

Krystal's anger flared. "What's he doing out there?"

"No clue," Samuel chimed in. "We couldn't wake him."

While the others fretted over Matthew, Wilma remained less concerned, eager to share the wonderful news about the new babies with Ada and Samuel.

Curiosity getting the better of her, Krystal cautiously moved to the living room window and pulled aside the curtain. All she could see was a figure entirely enveloped in a sleeping bag.

Meanwhile, Samuel stepped outside, joining Obadiah as they examined the porch railing together.

A minute later, Obadiah's hammer produced a resounding bang that jolted Matthew awake. He sat up and looked around, his hair sticking out in all directions.

Krystal quickly retreated, releasing her grip on the curtains to avoid being seen.

Jed approached her. "What are you going to do?"

She turned to face him. "This is on a whole new level. It was easier when he was just following me. Now I don't know what to do."

"He's best ignored. Eventually, he'll give up and move on," Jed advised.

Krystal nervously bit her lip. "Maybe. I don't understand why he won't leave me alone."

"He's certainly determined. I'll give him that. It's as if you've cast a spell on him," Jed said playfully.

"Don't even joke about it. He knows you're here. It's unbelievable that he's trying to drive a wedge between us. I've made it clear that there's no hope. He and I never truly had a relationship. He hasn't lost anything because we never had anything substantial."

Jed nodded. "I believe you."

Realizing how she must have sounded, Krystal quickly apologized. "I'm sorry, but he infuriates me. This isn't my usual behavior."

Jed put his arm around her shoulders, offering support, and just then Ada's voice called out from the kitchen. "Come and have breakfast, you two. Don't worry about him out there. He'll eventually move on."

"See, even she agrees," Jed whispered to Krystal. They walked into the kitchen and took their seats at the table.

"Is Matthew really sleeping through all that noise?" Debbie asked Krystal.

"He was asleep until the hammering started." Krystal handed Jed a plate for himself. He filled it with food before placing it in front of her.

Debbie noticed the considerate gesture and smiled at Krystal, who smiled back gratefully. Matthew had never served her food before, so she appreciated Jed's kindness.

Ada shook her head, expressing her complete disapproval. "Matthew's really making a fool of himself. I can't imagine what my dear sister would say. I don't think I'll tell her about this. She'd immediately send for him and demand he come home."

Krystal silently agreed with that idea but chose not to voice her opinion. Other than his persistent harassment, she held no personal grudge against Matthew.

"Why is he out there?" Debbie frowned.

"Who knows?" Wilma replied, taking a sip of the coffee that Debbie had prepared. She then added, "Desperate people often resort to desperate measures."

"I apologize for my nephew's behavior, Jed. This isn't typical of him. I'm embarrassed for him, as well as for myself," Ada said.

Jed offered her a sympathetic smile. "No need to apologize. I can understand his problem. It's not easy to mend a broken heart."

Krystal cast a sideways glance at Jed, her mind suddenly buzzing with unasked questions. He had unfolded many chapters of his life to her, yet the pages of past heartbreak remained untouched and unread. She could sense a hidden depth in his silence, a story untold perhaps?

CHAPTER 3

"*W*here is Matthew?" Jared asked from his small table in the corner of the room.

"Never mind," Debbie told him. "Finish your breakfast so you can grow up big and strong."

"Jed, don't put yourself in his shoes because you don't know the history! He has no one to blame but himself for how things have turned out." Ada spooned some scrambled eggs onto her plate.

Suddenly, Samuel entered the room holding something in front of him with his fingertips. Ada noticed and furrowed her brow. "What is that, Samuel?"

"Krystal, Matthew asked me to give this to you." He held the white handkerchief out to her.

Krystal scrunched up her nose. "He wants me to have that?"

"I think it's a letter of some kind. He wrote something on it," Samuel said.

Ada stuck her nose in the air. "I only hope it's a clean handkerchief."

Krystal hesitated, then finally reached out to take it. Samuel then went back outside. Krystal didn't want Jed to be jealous, so she felt compelled to read it aloud. "Dear Krystal, I will wait here until you are finished with that guy. Sigrid was never the one for me, and soon you will understand Jed isn't right for you either. Love, forever and a day, Matthew."

"Ach, this is embarrassing," Ada moaned.

"Forever and a day, eh?" Wilma chuckled.

Jed sat rigid in his chair, his gaze fixed on the untouched food on his plate. A heavy silence hung around him, isolating him from the conversation.

With a flick of her wrist, Krystal tossed the handkerchief onto the table. It landed with a soft flutter, and she let out a sigh. "He's just going to hang around the porch and hope Jed and I break up? It's hard enough seeing him around, and now I will have to see him whenever I go outside."

Jed shifted forward in his chair. "Shall I ask him to leave?"

"No," Krystal said, her voice low and laced with concern. "He's already teetering on the edge, isn't he? And lately... his behavior is more eccentric than usual." She wrung her hands.

"Mamm, can I go see Matthew?" Jared's eyes opened wide.

"Not right now."

"He's my best friend. That's so unfair!" Jared crossed his arms and huffed.

Ada stared at Jared, shaking her head. "In my day, children didn't talk like that." Ada leaned over to Debbie and whispered, "Don't worry, he'll do a lot better when you get married. He needs a strong male in his life to make him behave. It doesn't help that he's the only child in the household either."

Debbie gave a noncommittal nod, her gaze shifting away from Ada's as a clear sign she wished to end the conversation.

"He's your best friend, Jared? I thought Fritz was your best friend," Wilma said.

"No. He's *Dat*. He will be soon. Matthew's my best friend for now."

"We'll see Matthew later. Just finish your breakfast," Debbie told him.

"Everyone, I think this is the best plan. When you go outside, don't pay Matthew any mind. Act like he doesn't exist," Ada stated. "He's doing it for attention, so let's not give him any. He'll have to start work soon, so he'll be gone, and I'm sure he won't return for another night in the cold on the hard wooden planks of the porch." Ada piled more eggs onto her plate as she shook her head in disgust.

Krystal bit her lip, worry creasing her brow. "We're just going to walk past him like it's normal for someone to sleep on someone else's porch, uninvited?"

"Exactly," Ada said as she popped a forkful of eggs into her mouth.

"What do you two have planned for today?" Debbie asked Jed and Krystal to lighten the mood.

"I'm working in the morning, and then Bliss is working for me in the afternoon so Jed and I can spend time together."

Jed grinned. "Sounds good to me. Wilma, if there's anything you need help with around here this morning, I'd be more than happy to pitch in."

"Thank you, Jed. Maybe Samuel or Obadiah need help with something."

"I'll ask them." He went to stand up, but Wilma insisted he finish his breakfast first.

When it was time to leave for work, Krystal stood up and sighed. "Well, this is going to be awkward, walking past Matthew."

"I'll be with you. I'll hitch your buggy for you," Jed said.

"Thank you."

"We'll follow you out. Ready for school, Jared?" Debbie asked.

"Do I have to go?" he whined as he set his plate on the kitchen bench.

"You can see Matthew when you leave," Ada suggested.

"Yay! Let's go, *Mamm!*"

"Wasn't the plan to ignore him?" Debbie frowned at Ada.

"Do you want Jared to leave for school or not?" Ada shrugged.

"Okay."

Jed and Krystal walked to the front door together while Debbie placed Jared's bag onto his shoulders.

"Remember, he's not even there," a voice from the kitchen rang out. Both Krystal and Debbie exchanged a bewildered look. Ada was contradicting herself. Or was she implying that Jared was the only one allowed to interact with Matthew?

When Debbie opened the door, she saw Matthew was helping Obadiah and Samuel as they worked on the porch railing. His sleeping bag was carelessly left in the middle of the porch, and his white shirt was dreadfully creased and not tucked into his pants.

Matthew straightened up to look at them, but none of them uttered a word as each of them strolled past him.

"Hi, Matthew!" Jared called out, giving him a friendly wave.

"Enjoy your day at school, Jared." Matthew watched them with a smile that quickly faded as he saw the others move past him without a word. Despite the cold reception, he clung to his conviction—it was only a matter of time before he and Krystal found their way back to each other.

Each glance Krystal shared with Jed was a sting, a reminder of the place he'd once held not only in her life but also within his circle of friends and family.

CHAPTER 4

*A*nxiety prickling at her skin, Favor raked her eyes across the local gazette, searching fervently for the 'For Lease' section. Her in-laws were in desperate need of a place to call their own but not as desperate as Favor was to find one for them.

Nothing. Not even a simple advertisement for a bed and breakfast. There had to be a place for them, somewhere they could lay their heads for a while.

Feeling the weight of her fruitless search, Favor set aside the paper. Her fingers fidgeted with the strings of her *kapp*, mirroring the worry that gnawed at her insides.

She moved to the kitchen window, her gaze sweeping over the outside world while her mind raced, hoping for a plan. Without one, Harriet and Melvin would be homeless, and the alternative was them overstaying their welcome in her home.

Inhaling deeply, she willed her thoughts to still. She couldn't let her personal feelings guide her actions. Despite the tension, Harriet and Melvin were Simon's parents. They had a hand in molding the man she loved, and that made it her duty to help them.

But the bitter pill was easier to swallow when she pictured helping her own mother instead. A pang of longing twisted in her chest as she thought of her mother back home at the orchard. She missed her deeply.

Tears threatened at the corners of her eyes, but she quickly wiped away the single tear that escaped. Self-pity was not the route to take. She had to be strong for Simon. He had eventually made the tough choice of distancing himself from his parents for their own good.

Melvin and Harriet had at least tried to be useful during their stay, staying busy with household chores. Melvin helped Simon clear out the spare bedroom while Harriet took up the task of sweeping and dusting every nook and cranny. But Harriet's relentless cleaning left Favor feeling as if her own housekeeping efforts were never quite enough.

Suddenly, a cheerful greeting rang out from outside, snapping Favor out of her gloominess. She recognized the voice in an instant – Cherish. Favor felt a wave of relief wash over her at the sound of her sister's voice.

As she moved to let Cherish in, Harriet unexpectedly beat her to it. Harriet enveloped Cherish in a warm embrace, only releasing her to give Malachi the same treatment.

Cherish's eyebrows rose in surprise at seeing Harriet and Melvin. When they told her about their situation and their search for a home, she turned to Favor, her gaze probing for a reaction.

Despite her surprise, Harriet seemed to effortlessly take over Favor's home, offering seats and drinks to their guests. Favor felt left out, unable to voice her discomfort without risking rudeness.

"We had no idea you'd be here," Cherish confessed, her eyes darting between Harriet and Favor. "I need to tell you we got a phone call from Earl. The twins have been born, both boys."

Favor screamed and then clapped a hand over her mouth. "I'm so happy for them. And for us. When can we see them?"

"I'm not sure. Earl said he'd visit *Mamm*, but he wasn't sure when."

"We'll have to visit at the same time, all of us," Favor said.

Cherish nodded. "He also said that Miriam's fine and the babies are both healthy. And, we've also brought over a bed for your spare room. I'm guessing that will come in handy."

Harriet clapped her hands together, a pleased look on her face. "Oh, that's just what we need. Your bed is so uncomfortable, Favor."

Favor bit back a response, choosing instead to press

her lips into a thin line. The criticism stung, especially considering that she and Simon had given up their bed for the in-laws, resigning themselves to the living room.

Then Melvin chimed in, declaring that they didn't need any refreshments and that the men would get the bed from the wagon.

Once the men were gone, and Cherish and Favor were alone, Cherish whispered, "Why are they here?"

Favor let out a sigh. "They just showed up. They didn't even wait to sell their farm. They found someone to lease it. They got here yesterday."

Cherish's eyebrows drew together in sympathy. "I'm sorry. Did you hear what Harriet said about the bed? Seriously, there's nothing wrong with your bed. It seems nothing's good enough for her. She's already acting as if she owns the place. It wouldn't occur to her that you might not agree with her views. They could stay at our place. We have plenty of bedrooms."

"Thanks, but they have agreed to find a place. They know they can't stay here."

"That's something, at least."

Their conversation was interrupted by Harriet's re-entry with mugs of hot tea, followed by an array of cookies Harriet had brought with her. Harriet continued to express her delight at being with Favor and Simon, believing it to be God's will.

Favor stifled her annoyance as Harriet began assessing their home and planning improvements. Even when Cherish tried to ease the situation, Harriet ignored her. The conversation was a clear display of Harriet's meddling nature, and Favor became increasingly desperate to find them a place to live. The sooner, the better.

However, Cherish's support and encouragement brought Favor some relief. She was reminded that this time, she wasn't alone in dealing with Harriet and Melvin.

CHAPTER 5

avor glanced at Harriet. "What are your plans for the next few days?"

Leaning back in her chair, Harriet paused for a moment. "Well, I thought I'd take a good look at your land—maybe even have a stroll around it. And perhaps we could go into town and do some shopping. I need to pick up a few things for this house to brighten it up a little."

Favor dreaded the thought. Harriet loved to scour second-hand shops looking for bargains, which was the last thing Favor wanted to do.

Cherish chimed in. "Looks like this little house will be rather crowded for the next little while."

Harriet nodded in agreement. "Yes, it certainly will be. It's far too small for a family. I'm glad you're planning to extend it, Favor. We're not going to be here long, Cherish, not in this house. We're on the lookout for a place to lease."

"I'll ask around. It shouldn't take long to find something," Cherish said.

Harriet seemed rather pleased with the idea, a faint smile dancing on her lips. "If this house was bigger, you could have a proper nursery. I'd be more than happy to lend you a hand. I have quite a knack for design, layouts, and such. And when the time comes, Pa can make a crib. Or better yet, we could fetch Simon's crib from our attic back home. We moved most of our belongings into the attic, and some other things are stored in one of the sheds."

Favor cringed inwardly at the thought of an ancient, probably unsafe crib that Harriet had most likely found at some flea market. Favor found her voice, gently but firmly setting the boundary. "I appreciate both offers, but I'd like to be the one to arrange the baby's room when the time comes."

Harriet seemed to shrug off the rebuff, her attention turning to Cherish. "And what about you, Cherish? Any babies on the horizon?"

Cherish responded with a teasing smile. "None that I know of. I'll keep an eye out though."

A hint of confusion crossed Harriet's face. "Keep an eye out?"

"Yes," Cherish replied, her eyes twinkling with mischief. "I'll keep an eye on the horizon. If I see a baby, I'll go and collect it."

Harriet's confusion turned into a mild exasperation. "I hope that's a joke."

Cherish responded with a chuckle. "Don't worry, Harriet. I'm well aware of the facts of life."

Harriet's features softened. "That's a relief. When I was a girl, I was told that storks brought the babies." She added with a sigh, "Mind you, it would be a lot easier if storks did deliver the children. Childbirth is no picnic, you know."

Favor merely nodded, not eager to dwell on the prospect of childbirth. She took another sip of tea, the warmth soothing her nerves.

"It's a big responsibility, having children," Harriet mused. "But I have faith that you and Simon will make wonderful parents. And I'll be here to help in any way I can."

"Thank you, Harriet," Favor replied, touched by the sincerity in her mother-in-law's voice. Her mother-in-law did come in handy sometimes, but not very often.

As Harriet sipped her tea, her gaze bounced between Favor and Cherish. "Perhaps you could both enjoy an outing together. Favor and I will have plenty of opportunities to catch up, Cherish, if you and Favor want to do something by yourselves."

Catching Favor's pleading look, Cherish knew she had to come up with something. "We could go for a walk. It's such a lovely day."

Harriet nodded approvingly, standing and stretching

her arms. "That sounds delightful. Do you mind if I join you if that's all you're doing?"

"Of course, you can," Favor said. "Shall we head out?"

With Harriet leading the way, Favor and Cherish stepped into the warmth of the sun. Nature unfurled itself before them, painting a picture of serene beauty. Wildflowers lent their sweetness to the air, while the distant chirping of birds created a melodic backdrop to their walk.

The peaceful atmosphere stirred something within Favor, soothing her worries. Cherish, too, seemed affected, her steps light and carefree. Harriet, however, remained quiet. Her brow furrowed, she appeared lost in her thoughts, a stark contrast to the sunny surroundings.

Concern nudged Favor. "Is everything okay, Harriet?"

Harriet offered a weak smile. "Yes, everything's fine. Just thinking something over."

Favor got straight to the point. "Well, what is it?"

Harriet took a deep breath and stopped walking. "I'm just worried about Simon," she said, her voice barely above a whisper.

Alarm bells rang in Favor's head as she asked, "Worried about Simon? Why?" A knot of worry began to take shape in her stomach.

Harriet didn't meet her gaze. "I see how he looks at you. The love he has for you is clear for anyone to see.

But I fear that he may not be able to give you the most important thing."

Caught off guard, Favor asked, "What do you mean?"

Harriet's eyes met hers then, heavy with unspoken fears. "I mean, children. You wish to start a family, and what if Simon is incapable of that? What if he inherited some genetic problem from me that makes him unable to have any children?"

Quick to settle her mother-in-law's fears, Favor said, "I don't believe it works that way, Ma. Don't worry. Let's be patient. I have faith that we'll have a family of our own."

Harriet's eyes softened, but worry still lurked in them. "I just want the best for both of you. I hate the thought of seeing either of you suffer."

"Trust me, Harriet... I mean, Ma," Favor reassured her. "We will handle whatever challenges life throws at us. If God doesn't bless us with children, we will find happiness elsewhere. We're still young, with plenty of time ahead of us. There's no need for worry."

Harriet heaved a sigh, her shoulders dropping slightly. "I know. I just can't help being this way."

Favor's heart softened, and she reached over and took Harriet's hand, offering a comforting squeeze. "It's okay to worry but don't let it consume you. One day, our house will echo with the laughter of our children. I just know it."

At Favor's words, Harriet's eyes sparkled. "That would be an absolute joy."

Favor's heart warmed at Harriet's enthusiasm. However, before she could reply, Cherish piped up, her voice enthusiastic. "I have a story to share."

Harriet's turned to Cherish. "Oh? Please, go on. I love a good story."

"It's a true story. My older half-brother, Earl, married a woman older than him."

Harriet's eyebrows rose. "The one who just had twins?"

"Yes, the very same. Despite her age and all the negativity she got from people, she now has..." Cherish counted on her fingers. "She now has seven children."

Delight etched itself across Harriet's face. "That's remarkable!"

"Never say never. Because it's never too late," Cherish said.

Tears welled in Harriet's eyes, a hand finding its way to her heart. "Such a blessing. They must be overjoyed."

Cherish nodded, a soft smile on her lips. "Truly. Miracles occur, Harriet. Favor and Simon have a lifetime ahead of them, filled with possibilities."

Nodding slowly, Harriet looked thoughtful. "Perhaps you're right. I'm just anxious for them. I don't wish for them to suffer as I did. Yet, maybe, I should trust in God's timing and find peace in faith."

Favor felt a swell of gratitude for Cherish's words

and the hopeful light they seemed to shine in Harriet's eyes. "Thank you, Harriet. We will take it one day at a time and trust in God."

With that, they turned to walk back to the house, the morning sun casting long shadows on the path. As they strolled through the grassy trail, Favor slipped her arm around Harriet in a supportive embrace while Cherish did the same to Favor, their unity casting a warm glow on the path ahead.

CHAPTER 6

On Tuesday, the kitchen was a flurry of activity as Wilma and Ada collaborated with Susan and Daphne to bake a variety of sample cakes for Debbie's wedding. The delightful aroma of vanilla, chocolate, and raspberry wafted from the oven, saturating the room with sweet scents.

They were keen to have Debbie's nod of approval on each one before it got onto the wedding menu.

Ada filled her lungs with the scent, her eyes closing momentarily. "There's no aroma quite like cakes baking."

"It is comforting," Wilma agreed, pressing a tiny raspberry onto a dollop of frosting on a chocolate mud cake before moving onto the next.

"Isn't it delightful, cooking together like this?" Susan asked, her smile lighting up the room.

"It is. Wilma and I cook together almost every day,"

Ada announced, her hand moving rhythmically as she mixed a bowl of chocolate frosting.

"The wedding must be causing excitement in your house, Wilma. It's not far off now, is it?" Daphne carefully slid a cake tin into the preheated oven.

Ada looked at Wilma for confirmation. "We're quite looking forward to it, aren't we, Wilma?"

"Exactly when is the big day?" Susan pushed her glasses up on her nose, a curious tilt to her head.

Ada threw a glance at Wilma before responding, "Well, they haven't pinned down an exact date yet."

"Still no date? People will need to know, especially if they're traveling from far away," Daphne blurted out.

"All we know is it's going to be before Christmas. Debbie will tell us as soon as she knows." Wilma found it curious that there wasn't a set date yet. She pondered whether she should urge Debbie to press Fritz again for a date, considering all the preparations required.

"I'm sure they'll figure out a date soon," Susan commented before reaching for one of the tiny cakes and popping it into her mouth.

Taken aback, Ada exclaimed, "Susan! Those are for Debbie!"

Caught mid-chew, Susan apologetically removed the half-eaten cake from her mouth and placed it back on the plate. "My apologies. That one just looked too tempting."

"No, it's my fault for leaving it where you could swoop in on it," Ada swiftly responded, playfully waving her wooden spoon at Susan. "There's only one red velvet cake for Debbie to sample, so finish that one. I'll whip up another. I might have to hide it in the cupboard."

Susan finished the rest of the cake, looking somewhat relieved.

"There's no need for any fuss." Wilma extended a tray of miniature cakes toward Susan. "Help yourself to one of these."

Daphne was still concerned about Debbie. "Have Debbie and Fritz decided where they'll live? Are they moving in with Fritz's mother?"

Wilma offered a shrug. "Your guess is as good as mine. I'm guessing they'll settle here at the orchard with me. At least that's what I'm hoping."

Ada broke into a chuckle at this, causing Wilma to pause in her task of wiping crumbs from the table.

Wilma stared at her best friend. "Why are you laughing?"

"Fritz isn't a teenager, Wilma," Ada pointed out, a teasing gleam in her eyes. "He's not some inexperienced juvenile. He won't be keen on living here with you and Krystal. No, no, no."

Susan nodded in agreement. "I think Ada is right. He's a grown man."

A genuine smile spread across Ada's face at Susan's affirmation.

"Perhaps Fritz already has a place in mind—a fresh start for their new life together," Daphne speculated.

"For Debbie's sake, I hope so," Wilma said, her gaze distant.

Wilma's friends had brought up some new ideas that now turned into worries. Soon Debbie would be leaving the house. But for Debbie's sake, it had to happen, and Wilma was eager to help Debbie and Fritz in any way she could.

Suddenly, the phone in the barn cut through the air, pulling Wilma from her thoughts. "The phone!" Wiping her flour-dusted hands on her apron, she darted outside toward the barn.

As always, the ring stopped just as her hand reached for the receiver. She sighed, leaning against the cool wall of the barn as she caught her breath.

Just as she had hoped, the phone blared into life once more. She picked up the receiver swiftly, breathlessly saying, "Hello?"

"Wilma, it's Carter. We're at the hospital."

Wilma's heart pounded in her chest. "What happened?" she asked, her hand instinctively flying to her heart.

Carter chuckled softly on the other end of the line. "Nothing to worry about. We have a baby. Florence gave birth late last night."

CHAPTER 7

"*W*hat?" Wilma's voice shook with the intensity of her joy. "Are they both okay?"

"Everything went perfectly. Florence and the baby are both doing splendidly. I was hoping you could stop by our place this afternoon to meet him."

"A boy?" Wilma gasped, excitement reverberating in her voice. "Miriam and Earl also had boys."

"I know," Carter replied, amusement clear in his voice. "This afternoon, is that alright? Florence will be discharged by then."

"She's leaving the hospital already?" Despite her initial shock, understanding dawned on Wilma. "I suppose it does make sense. Hospitals aren't the most comfortable places to rest."

"Exactly. They only need to watch her for a few

hours, they said. And we've hired a night nurse to help us over the next few weeks."

"I didn't realize time was passing so quickly." Wilma felt a pang of guilt. It was challenging to be there for all her family members. Her relationship with Florence had been strained before, and she didn't want it to go down that path again. "Congratulations. I'm overjoyed beyond words."

Carter chuckled. "I know the feeling. You're the first person I called."

"Thank you. Will you inform everyone else, or do you want me to call some people?"

"I'll do it. I've got the list right here. We'll be back home around three."

"I'll be there. We could use more boys in the family." Remembering that she forgot to inquire about the names of Earl's twins, she asked, "Have you decided on a name?"

"Not yet. We're letting Iris choose the name."

"Why would you do that?" Wilma blurted out.

"We want her to feel involved."

Wilma tried to express her support for the idea, although she thought it was unwise to assign such a responsibility to a young child. "What an interesting idea!"

"I must be going, but I'll see you this afternoon," Carter said.

"I'll be there. Congratulations again, and please send my love to Florence."

"Will do. Thanks, Wilma."

Wilma replaced the receiver and hurriedly ran into the house, desperate to share the news with the others. "I'm a grandmother again! Florence has just given birth."

"How wonderful!" Daphne exclaimed.

"Don't keep us in suspenders, Wilma. Is it a boy or a girl?" Ada asked.

"A boy," Wilma answered.

Daphne laughed and put her hand over her mouth. "I think you mean 'in suspense,' Ada, not suspenders."

Ada laughed. "Oh, that's right. I'm so delighted I can't even speak."

They all laughed at Ada, and a more joyous mood filled the room.

"How precious! What's his name?" Susan asked in between licking a spoon covered in frosting.

Wilma inhaled deeply. "This is the thing… they're letting Iris choose the name."

Ada scoffed. "Now, wait. I know I had trouble talking just now. Is the same thing happening to you, Wilma?"

Wilma looked over at Ada. "What do you mean?"

"Did you mean to say just now that Iris is choosing the baby's name?" Ada stared at Wilma.

Wilma shrugged her shoulders. "That's what I was told. They are allowing Iris to name her brother. Can you imagine that?"

Ada grunted her disapproval. "That's completely ridiculous. I've never heard of anything like it!"

Wilma was pleased that Ada shared her disgust over a child naming another child. Ada and she rarely disagreed on anything and that's why they were such good friends. "I completely agree."

Susan lifted her shoulders in a shrug. "I think it's sweet. It will make her feel closer to him. It makes me feel warm all over."

Ada glanced over at Susan. "You should've worn a summer dress if you feel warm." Ada shook her head.

"I mean warm on the inside."

"I think Ada knew what you meant," Daphne told Susan.

"Oh." Susan looked down.

"No! I don't like it at all. Iris will come up with a silly name, and then they'll have to tell her they can't possibly call the baby such a ridiculous name, and the poor child will be heartbroken. They shouldn't put such a huge burden on the small child. What would a child know about such things?"

"She might choose a good name," Daphne suggested.

Ada stuck her nose in the air. "We'll wait and see. Anyway, it's not my problem. I have enough problems trying to sort out my nephew's relationships with women."

"We have lots of clothes for the baby anyway, what-ever his name will be. If the name ends up being a little unusual, we'll get used to it." Wilma looked over at the baby clothes in the basket in the corner of the room. "Thank you all for your help making the clothes."

Ada's lips turned down at the corners. "They've got enough money to buy a whole department store full of clothes."

Wilma smiled. "I know, but Florence will appreciate these because they've been made with love."

"Ah, that's lovely, Wilma," Susan said.

Ada shook her head.

"We had a lot of fun sewing them. We always have fun over here, don't we, Susan?" Daphne asked.

"We do. I look forward to my days here at the orchard with all of you."

CHAPTER 8

$\mathcal{T}$he freshly picked flowers in Wilma's hand swayed gently as she and Ada waited at Florence and Carter's door. Ada held onto the basketful of clothes they'd made for the baby. At the sound of approaching footsteps, they straightened, huge smiles on their faces as Carter swung the door open, greeting them with a broad grin.

"Congratulations!" Ada and Wilma chorused, and Carter's grin widened as he accepted the flowers and the basket of clothes.

"Thank you. We couldn't be happier. Please, come in and meet your grandson, Wilma, and your new..." He hesitated, unsure what title to give Ada.

"I'll call him my great nephew, seeing as I'm like a sister to Wilma," Ada filled the silence smoothly.

"Aunt Ada it is, then," Carter said.

They followed Carter into the living room, where

Florence cradled the tiny baby in her arms. She looked up as they entered, her tired face glowing with a serene smile. "Hi."

Wilma's throat tightened as she gazed at the young woman holding her child. "I'm so pleased for you, Florence." She blinked back the tears that threatened to fall. She wished desperately that Florence's father could see his grandchildren.

"Thank you for the flowers," Florence said, having spotted them in Carter's hands.

Ada announced, "And Susan, Daphne, Wilma, and I all sewed the baby some clothes."

"Thank you. They'll come in handy. Be sure to thank Susan and Daphne for me. I rarely see them these days."

"We will," Ada said, stepping forward with Wilma to peer at the baby.

Florence pulled back the shawl to reveal the baby's peaceful face. "He's sleeping."

Wilma got a closer look and was struck by the resemblance. He looked just like Carter had as a baby. "He's beautiful. Isn't he, Ada?"

Ada leaned over Florence's shoulder. "He's red, wrinkly, and adorable," she declared just as the baby's eyes flickered open. A second later, he yelled.

Florence chuckled softly. "I think he's hungry." She adjusted her position to feed him.

Wilma looked around before she sat down. "Where's Iris?"

"She's sleeping upstairs," Carter answered. "Tea? Coffee?"

"Tea for us, please," Wilma said.

Ada joined Wilma on the couch, giving them a perfect view of the infant now feeding contentedly in Florence's arms.

There was no denying it, Wilma thought fondly. He was the most adorable baby she'd ever seen.

Memories swelled within Wilma, of holding a newborn Carter in her arms, of never wanting to let go. An ache echoed through her heart, a torrent of emotions threatening to spill forth. She blinked rapidly, fighting to keep her composure. She'd worked so hard over the years to keep walls around her heart.

Florence looked down at her son, a tender smile touching her lips. "He's asleep again," she said quietly, meeting Wilma's eyes. "Would you like to hold him?"

"Thank you, Florence." Wilma's voice was thick with unshed tears. As Florence gently placed the baby in her arms, Wilma took a moment to bask in the warmth and softness of the newborn.

Before long, Ada became impatient. "My turn, Wilma! I hardly ever see my own grandchildren since they live so far away. It's been ages since I held a tiny baby."

Wilma looked up to see Ada staring at the baby, but she clutched him a little tighter. "Just another minute, Ada."

Florence chuckled softly, observing the interaction. "You really love newborns, don't you, Ada?"

"I do." Ada grinned, and then frowned slightly. "Why is Iris asleep at this hour?"

"She stayed up for the birth, so she hasn't had much sleep," Florence answered calmly.

Ada gasped, her hand flying to her mouth. "There for the birth? She saw everything?"

Florence's laughter filled the room. "Just part of it," she replied. Ada's shocked expression seemed to amuse her even more. "Relax, Ada. It's part of our parenting approach. We want Iris included in everything. We believe it'll make her a more well-rounded person if we treat her as an adult."

Wilma barely registered the exchange. She was lost in the baby's peaceful features.

Ada, however, was less than impressed. She made a face yet remained silent. She had seen the changes in Florence ever since she'd met Carter. Ada sighed inwardly, wishing that Carter had joined their community rather than Florence leaving. She forced a smile. "Well, you don't look like you just gave birth. You look like you've had a relaxing day at the park."

Florence gave a wry smile. "I can assure you, I don't feel like it. I'm sore, and I'm tired."

Wilma finally looked up, meeting Ada's eyes. "Okay, it's your turn, Ada," she said, gently passing the baby over.

Florence began to stand, but both Ada and Wilma urged her back into her seat.

"What a beautiful baby! Such a lovely child ought to have a lovely name." Ada paused, pretending she didn't know they were allowing Iris to name him. "Has he got a name yet?"

Florence's face softened. "Iris is still thinking it over. She'll come up with a name soon."

Ada glanced at Wilma, a teasing smile playing on her lips. "An excellent idea, don't you think, Wilma?"

Wilma nodded, leaning forward with excitement. "I can't wait to hear what she comes up with!"

Their banter drew a soft giggle from Florence just as Carter reappeared in the room with a tray bearing tea and cookies. As he set it on the coffee table, Wilma glanced at him, an idea dawning on her.

"Carter," she started. "You know those houses Levi left me that you're looking after?"

"Yes." Carter nodded, settling himself on the armrest of Florence's chair.

"I was thinking... Debbie and Fritz are getting married soon, and they need a home. Could we arrange for them to live in one of those houses?" Wilma's question hung in the air, a potential solution to her earlier concern about where Debbie and Fritz would live.

Carter's eyebrows rose. "That's very generous of you, Wilma. Do you want to rent it to them or give it to them?"

Wilma shrugged. "Debbie was Levi's niece. I think it's only fair to offer the house to them as a gift."

"Alright." Carter nodded thoughtfully. "One of the houses had storm damage, but repairs are almost done. It should be ready in about a month."

"Perfect timing." Wilma was satisfied that it was all meant to be.

"Wait," Ada interjected, her eyebrows furrowed, "no one's living there currently?"

Carter shook his head, "The repairs were extensive. We had to move the previous tenants out. The house has been vacant for a few months now."

"Where is it located?" Wilma asked.

"It's not far. Just down the road. It's the white house with the red roof."

Wilma knew the one. It was also not far from the orchard. "It's small, but it'll be enough for the three of them. At least it'll be a good start for them."

"Wilma, you show such kindness," Florence said, touching her heart. "What an amazing thing to do for Debbie."

"Well, Levi would've wanted it. He was very close to Debbie. He stepped into his brother's shoes and became like a father to Debbie."

"I'll contact my attorney to draft all the necessary paperwork," Carter said.

"You can arrange it all?" Wilma asked.

"Of course. I'll get the ball rolling, and hopefully,

you'll be able to gift the house to them before their wedding."

Ada let out an impressed whistle as she returned the baby to Florence. "That's quite the wedding present," she remarked.

Wilma ignored Ada's opinion. "Thank you, Carter, for looking after the houses. It's too much for me to manage."

Florence spoke before Carter could reply. "It gives him something to do."

Carter chuckled. "I do enjoy it."

Wilma looked down at the baby again. "He looks just like you, Carter."

Carter grinned. "That's what we thought too."

"Have you told everyone? Wilma and I weren't sure if you had spread the news yet, so we only informed Susan and Daphne since they were there when you called."

Carter nodded. "I called everyone who lives far away. I spoke to Cherish, and she'll let Favor know. Then I called Florence's sisters up north. However, I haven't been able to reach Debbie and Krystal."

"We'll tell them," Wilma said.

"I also spoke to Earl. He's a very busy man," Carter chuckled.

"He certainly would be with seven youngsters. We should leave and let you both rest," Ada said.

Florence glanced over at the barely touched tea.

"But you haven't even finished your tea. Please, stay awhile."

Wilma felt heartened. "Are you sure?"

"Of course. The nurse is coming soon, and when she takes the baby, we'll both have a chance to rest."

CHAPTER 9

*A*s the women sipped their tea and nibbled on cookies, Florence felt a sudden wave of exhaustion. She had been awake for too long, and her sore body started protesting. She reclined on the couch with the baby in her arms, listening to Wilma and Ada's lively conversation.

An unfamiliar sense of longing washed over her. Though content with Carter, she missed her community. Sometimes she longed for the simplicity of life with them, the communal care they provided. She had left it all behind for love, and while she harbored no regrets, a twinge of desire for her days with Wilma and the girls at the house on the orchard occasionally resurfaced.

However, she knew she couldn't dwell on such things for too long. She now had a family of her own— a husband and two beautiful children. Her focus needed to be on building a different life with them. She clung to the hope that one day Carter might come to believe in a creator, to accept that God was real. She would never abandon that hope.

As the women finished their tea, the nurse arrived, providing Florence with an opportunity to rest. While Wilma and Ada stayed with the baby, Florence went to lie down for five minutes. She closed her eyes, letting the exhaustion engulf her as she drifted into a peaceful sleep.

Upon waking, she heard a distant conversation that told her that Ada and Wilma were still there.

Rising slowly and wincing at the pain in her body, she made her way to the door. As she opened it, the sound of laughter from the living room greeted her. A smile spread across her face, and she followed the joyful noise.

Upon entering the room, she found Carter and Ada on the couch, laughing over a shared joke. Wilma busied herself in the kitchen, tidying up the dishes. Florence's heart swelled with affection for these people, her family.

As she nestled on the other side of Carter, he draped his arm around her, drawing her into his side. She rested her head on his shoulder, relishing the warmth of his body.

"I love you," he murmured into her ear.

Florence responded with a smile, her heart aglow with warmth. "I love you too," she echoed softly.

Everything she desired was here in this moment. She let her eyes drift shut, tuning into the steady rhythm of Carter's heartbeat, Wilma's gentle humming from the kitchen, and Ada's comforting presence nearby.

Wilma came back into the room. "We should head out now. The kitchen's all set. If there's anything more you need, let us know. We're not far away."

"Yes, we better go. There's bound to be something stirring back at Wilma's," Ada added.

Wilma nodded in agreement. "No doubt there is."

"I'll give you a ride home to spare you the walk," Carter offered.

"Thank you, Carter. We'd appreciate that."

Several minutes later, Ada and Wilma huddled together in the driveway of the orchard, their eyes following Carter's car as it disappeared down the road.

"How are you holding up, Wilma?" Ada asked.

"I'm just grateful the baby arrived safely."

"Me too. You seem a bit down, though."

Wilma shook her head. "I can't help but wonder how my life would've turned out if I'd made different choices."

"Like if you'd raised Carter yourself?" Ada ventured.

Wilma nodded. "I know Josiah would've welcomed any child with open arms. He never cared about what anyone thought. He always made up his own mind about things. That was one of the things I loved about him."

Ada placed a comforting hand on Wilma's arm. "You need to stop torturing yourself with 'what ifs.' If you'd raised Carter, he and Florence would've grown up as step-siblings. Their marriage wouldn't have happened."

Wilma nodded, acknowledging Ada's valid point. "You're right, but it doesn't get rid of my feelings of guilt."

"Let's head inside, and I'll make you something comforting to eat."

Wilma gave a faint smile. Food was always Ada's solution to life's problems.

As they walked up the porch steps, Ada continued her pep talk, "You should know by now, mothers always find a way to feel guilty about something."

"That's the truth." Wilma inhaled deeply, appreciating Ada's unwavering support. Her friend had always been her rock during tough times. She knew she could rely on Ada to provide comfort and solace, no matter the circumstance.

Once inside the house, Ada immediately got to work in the kitchen while Wilma sank onto the couch. Reflecting on Ada's comment about maternal guilt, she couldn't help but dwell on her own mothering experience. She had endured many sleepless nights fretting over her children and the choices they made. Despite striving to be the best mother possible, there were times when she questioned if she had done enough.

The clamor of pots and pans in the kitchen interrupted her thoughts. Ada had started on dinner, and the aroma of something savory wafted through the air. Wilma's stomach rumbled, a reminder that she hadn't had a proper meal since breakfast. The cake tastings for Debbie's wedding and the cookies at Florence's house had been enjoyable but hardly satisfying.

Rising from the couch, Wilma made her way to the kitchen and watched as Ada moved with practiced ease around the large space. With fluid motions, she chopped vegetables and tended to simmering pots. It made Wilma marvel at how her friend could make everything appear so effortless.

"Who's coming for dinner tonight?" Wilma asked.

"I don't know. There could be someone we don't expect. What about Obadiah?"

"I didn't invite him. Not that I recall."

"Speaking about him, I'm still waiting on letters back from my friends. They'll answer my questions about Obadiah, and if he's hiding anything, he won't be hiding it for long."

Wilma put her hand over her mouth and chuckled. "Oh, Ada. He's not hiding anything. You're too suspicious."

"I hope you're right."

CHAPTER 10

avor had spent the entire night tossing and turning. She'd received the news that her half-sister, Florence, had a new baby. While she was happy for Florence and Carter, it made her feel worse about her childless situation. On top of yearning for a child, she was yet to free herself from Harriet and Melvin. Everything was oppressive.

She had imagined that having her own home would alleviate her worries and that everything else would fall into place. Sitting up in bed, she turned on the gas lamp and glanced at her husband. Simon was sound asleep, softly snoring.

No matter how hard Favor tried, she couldn't quiet her restless thoughts. Simon stirred and opened his eyes as she contemplated leaving the bed to prepare a snack.

He rolled over, propping himself up on his elbow.

"Sorry, did I wake you?" Favor asked.

"No, it's alright. Are you okay?"

"I'm fine. I just can't sleep."

He yawned. "Sorry we haven't had a chance to talk about it. I know you're upset."

Favor yearned to pour out her feelings to Simon, but she knew it would only upset him, and it wouldn't change anything. So, for the first time ever, she held back.

Simon had fulfilled his role as a good husband, supporting her when they left his parents' house. He wasn't the one to blame.

"I'm fine." She leaned over and gave him a quick kiss on the cheek.

Simon stared at her. "Are you sure?"

"Yes."

"I'll find them somewhere to stay tomorrow. I won't stop until I find them something."

"No," Favor whispered. "You'll have to keep them occupied while I visit the doctor tomorrow."

"You're right. We'll have to proceed with our plans. You don't look so well." Simon sat up, placing the back of his hand on her forehead. "You feel warm."

"I just need some sleep."

"I give you my word, they'll be gone soon. Please, don't worry."

Favor nestled into him. "You can't say that because it's out of your control, but thank you for the thought."

"Who knows? Perhaps soon, we'll have a little one

running around here. Ma might come in handy then. It would be nice to have someone help us when we need it, wouldn't it?"

Favor wasn't convinced. She was certain she could manage. Nonetheless, she meekly replied, "I suppose so."

Simon kissed her forehead, then leaned across her and turned off the light. "Good night." With a few comforting words from her husband, Favor finally drifted to sleep in his arms.

THE NEXT MORNING, Favor woke and instinctively reached for her coffee like she did every other day. Sitting up, she noticed the absence of both her coffee mug and Simon from the bed.

Frowning, she stretched her arms above her head and muttered, "What is going on?" She climbed out of bed and peered out the window. In the distance, she saw Simon building a fence under Melvin's supervision. Closer to the house, Harriet was busy digging in the dirt with a shovel.

With no inkling of what Harriet was up to and not particularly in the mood to find out, Favor decided to seize the opportunity to leave while everyone thought she was still asleep. She dressed quickly and stepped out of the bedroom. As she passed the kitchen, she noticed a plate covered in foil sitting on the table.

Could Harriet have left that for her? She tried to pass it by, but the tantalizing smell was irresistible.

She sat down and lifted the foil from the plate revealing Harriet's special breakfast. There were scrambled eggs with relish, two sausages, a slice of bacon, and a tiny saucer on the side filled with baked beans. Favor quickly devoured every single item on the plate.

Much as she hated to admit it, she realized that she had missed Harriet's cooking and appreciated not having to cook for once. Looking up at the clean kitchen benches, she realized everything had already been washed up and put away.

After finishing her meal, she put her dish in the sink, intending to leave the kitchen. But then, she remembered Harriet's rules about never leaving dirty dishes, and she hesitated. A thought crossed her mind. Was she washing this plate immediately because Harriet expected it? This was her house, not Harriet's. If she adhered to Harriet's demands, it would imply that Harriet was in charge.

In a subtle act of rebellion, Favor left the dish in the sink. Now, it was time to head to the doctor. She hoped she could be seen without an appointment.

CHAPTER 11

That night at the orchard, everyone gathered in the living room before dinner. Krystal sat beside Jed, and amidst the conversation, she noticed he was quieter than normal. "Are you alright?" she asked softly.

Jed paused before responding. "I'll be fine."

Krystal knew otherwise. "You can share your thoughts with me. Some people say I'm a good listener."

A small smile played on Jed's lips. "Is that so?" His shoulder lightly bumped hers.

Krystal reciprocated his smile. She loved his playful side.

Jed looked up and saw everyone was looking at him. "I guess everyone knows how I feel about Krystal. It's why I'm here, why I want to stay. But I need a job."

Wilma looked delighted. "You're staying on? That's wonderful news, Jed."

Ada joined in. "We'd be glad to have you at our house for as long as you want. Won't your brother miss you, though?"

"Thank you. I doubt it. Ruth is another matter. I'll have to tell her soon."

Samuel leaned forward. "What job are you considering?"

"Anything really. I'd love to be my own boss. Although, I'm unsure about what exactly I want to do. I want to do something where I'm interacting with people. A job that offers a sense of accomplishment."

Krystal suggested, "Ever thought about helping out at the orchard? Harvest time is approaching."

Wilma agreed, "We do need extra hands around now. Talk to Fairfax, the manager."

"I don't think there's enough room for Matthew and me here," Jed replied with a grin. "I'm happy to assist during harvest, as long as Matthew and I are apart. I mean, I can't work next to Matthew after everything he's done to Krystal. I should probably work on my forgiveness, but I'm not there yet."

"Have some cake, Jed," Ada offered, pushing a plate of leftover cake samples toward him.

"Uh- thanks," Jed responded, reluctantly accepting the plate.

An idea sparked in Krystal's mind. "What about giving tours of the orchard and around town?"

Ada's eyes lit up. "That would be a great idea!"

Samuel nodded. "Lots of tourists visit these parts."

Debbie chimed in. "We could ask Eddie, the beekeeper, about including a tour of his hives."

Krystal added, "I asked Eddie and his family years ago when I had the idea and they were open to tours." Suggestions started pouring in from everyone.

Jed rubbed his chin. "A tour guide? I like that — showing people the sights."

"You're terrific with people, Jed. It's a perfect fit," Ada said, picking a piece of cake off his plate.

Debbie glanced at the corner, noticing her son Jared wasn't there. She stood abruptly. "Has anyone seen Jared?"

Wilma looked around. "He was here a moment ago..."

"Yes, but he's a little explorer, Wilma," Ada replied.

"I'll look upstairs." Debbie rushed upstairs only to find his room empty. She hurried to the front door, thinking he might be outside with Matthew. Throwing the door open, relief washed over her when she saw Jared standing beside Matthew. But the presence of two unfamiliar men startled her.

It was too dark to recognize them until one turned around.

Her heart leaped. "Fritz!" She couldn't hide her surprise. Fritz closed the gap between them. "Hello, Debbie."

"What are you doing here?" She longed to hug him, but the presence of others held her back.

He chuckled. "I told you I'd be back."

Jared slipped his hand into Fritz's. *"Dat's* here, *Mamm."*

Debbie's heart warmed. "Yes, he is. It's wonderful to see you."

"Likewise," Fritz replied.

"Are you here to stay now?" Debbie inquired.

"No. I'm only back for a few days." It was then she noticed the other man — Peter, Fritz's brother, and her ex-boyfriend. The sight of him made her uneasy. "Peter?" She couldn't hide her surprise.

CHAPTER 12

*P*eter stepped closer, and the light from within the house bathed his face, revealing a smile. "Congratulations, Debbie. I hope my presence doesn't upset you. I wanted to assure you there are no hard feelings, and I'm happy for you and Fritz."

Caught off guard, Debbie managed a smile. "Thank you, Peter. No hard feelings on my side either."

"Why would there be hard feelings from your end?" Peter's question left Debbie speechless. She shrugged, glancing at Matthew, who sat cross-legged atop his sleeping bag in an oddly casual pose.

She knelt before Jared. "You gave me a scare. Why are you outside?"

"Matthew wanted hot chocolate."

Debbie scowled at Matthew, who sipped his drink as if he didn't have a care in the world. "You let Jared make it?"

"No, *Mamm,* I didn't touch the stove," Jared said loudly.

"I brought my own equipment," Matthew chimed in. "Jared just fetched me a mug."

Looking closer, Debbie noticed a small gas stove and a teakettle next to Matthew's sleeping bag. Exhaling a tired sigh, she said, "Next time, don't let Jared come out here without us knowing. He's not supposed to wander off."

"I understand. I'm truly sorry, Debbie."

Debbie felt a pang of sympathy for Matthew. She offered him a consoling smile before turning to Fritz and Peter. "Please, come inside. Everyone will be delighted to see you both," she said, her gaze lingering on Fritz. "Have you eaten? You're just in time for dinner."

"Our mother is waiting for us. I'll see you tomorrow, though," Fritz said.

Peter placed a hand on Fritz's shoulder. "Fritz, we've come a long way. At least stay for a meal with your soon-to-be wife."

Fritz almost grimaced. "Okay. Our mother will understand, I hope."

"I'm sure she will," Peter added.

Debbie wondered if the awkwardness in the air was why Fritz was reluctant to stay. "You don't have to stay if you're tired."

"We're fine," Peter insisted, answering for himself and Fritz.

"Come inside then." Debbie held the door open, ushering them in.

"Bye, all," Matthew's voice faded as the front door closed.

After overcoming the surprise of Fritz's arrival, Debbie and Krystal quickly prepared places at the table for the brothers.

"Fritz, we weren't expecting to see you so soon," Krystal said.

"Fritz wanted to surprise Debbie," Peter told everyone.

Krystal looked over at Jed and realized no one had introduced him. "Meet Jed, Malachi's brother. He showed up recently, giving me a surprise too."

"Nice to meet you." Fritz extended his hand toward Jed.

Peter interjected, "And I'm Peter, an old friend of Debbie's." Silence filled the room momentarily before he added, "My brother, Fritz, is her new companion."

"We're a bit more than that," Fritz remarked.

Debbie felt her cheeks redden but kept her eyes down.

"Nice to meet both of you," Jed said.

"Are you here for good now, Fritz?" Samuel asked.

"Just visiting for a few days. Debbie and I need to discuss wedding details," Fritz answered.

Debbie felt a spark of relief, hoping for a date for the wedding.

"A sensible move. Everyone's been asking about the wedding details," Samuel said.

The tension heightened when Ada asked, "So, Peter. How's Maisy?"

"She's doing well. We're set to marry before Debbie and Fritz."

"Wunderbaar," Samuel responded. "Marriage is the best decision a man can make."

A warm smile spread across Ada's face as she glanced at Samuel.

Conversations about marriage made Debbie uneasy, and she wished they could change the subject. But when she looked at Fritz, his comforting smile set her heart racing. She was sure she'd made the right choice in choosing Fritz, but Peter's presence was still a nagging discomfort.

DURING DINNER, the conversation shifted to more pleasant topics. They discussed the upcoming harvest, the new babies in the family, and the latest community gossip. Debbie was relieved when the tension in the room melted away, replaced by the comforting familiarity of her family and friends.

After dinner, Fritz and Debbie found a quiet corner in the living room to talk. Settled on the couch, their hands entwined, they immersed themselves in the details of their special day while the others respectfully lingered in the kitchen for privacy's sake.

Later that evening, as Fritz and Peter prepared to leave, Peter waited in the buggy while Debbie said goodbye to Fritz on the porch. Taking Fritz's hand, she led him to a secluded corner, away from Matthew's sight.

"I can hardly believe it," she confessed. "You're actually here!"

"Did I worry you?"

A small smile tugged at her lips. "Maybe a little bit."

"I'm sorry. I wanted to surprise you."

"And you certainly did!"

His fingers traced her cheek lightly, "I've missed you."

"Me too, so much more than you know."

"Will you be able to take some time off while I'm here?" he asked.

"I'll try to find a substitute for work tomorrow. It's late, but I'll make some calls."

"Is that a yes, or a maybe?"

Knowing she had to give Fritz priority, she nodded. "It's a yes. If I can't find anyone, I'm sure Ada and Wilma can pitch in."

"I'm sure you'll figure it out. I'll come back in the morning." Fritz leaned in to place a gentle kiss on her cheek, and she caught sight of Peter observing them from the buggy. She withdrew. "What's the matter?"

"Someone might see," she whispered.

"Was it awkward with Peter here?" Fritz asked.

"A bit, but he's your brother. It'll take some time to adjust."

Fritz smiled. "He's getting married soon. He wants us to share that same joy."

Debbie wasn't entirely sure of that. From Peter's subtle hints, she sensed an undercurrent of bitterness. "I'm glad to hear he's doing well."

"I'd better leave now. We've barely spent time with our mother. We arrived, exchanged quick greetings, hitched the buggy, and left." Fritz's parting smile set her heart fluttering. "See you tomorrow."

"Goodbye." She watched as Fritz climbed into the buggy, and then the sound of horse hooves faded into the night.

Left alone on the porch, she turned her gaze upward, admiring the night sky above her. Gratitude washed over her for Fritz's safe journey home to her, but the silent prayer was abruptly interrupted.

CHAPTER 13

"*D*ebbie? Can you bring me some water? It's freezing out here."

Debbie glanced at Matthew, huddled in his sleeping bag, his body shaking from the cold. She'd forgotten he was there. "How's water going to help you?"

"I'm gonna heat it up on my stove."

"You should go home, Matthew."

"I can't."

"Why not?" Debbie asked, stepping closer.

"If I leave, it'll be the end for Krystal and me. This is the grandest gesture I've ever made for someone, and I believe it shows how much she means to me."

A frown creased Debbie's forehead. "Matthew, don't get me wrong, but everyone is worried about you. Can't you see that?"

"Maybe, but I gotta do what I gotta do."

"Krystal has moved on. You need to do the same. Camping on her doorstep will not win her back, even if that were a possibility. If anything, it's driving her away."

Defiance flickered in Matthew's eyes as he shook his head at Debbie. "No need to worry about the water. I'll try to get some sleep." With that, Matthew drew the sleeping bag over his head and turned to face the wall.

"Use the tap on the side of the house." Debbie sighed heavily as she retreated into the warmth of her home. In the living room, she noticed a folded up blanket. She picked it up and took it out to Matthew, and placed it over him. He had his head covered, so he didn't even notice.

Debbie remained quiet and went back inside.

The moment Debbie entered the kitchen, all eyes turned to her. Picking up a tea towel she moved toward the sink to help Krystal with the dishes while Ada and Wilma cleared the table and brought over more dirty dishes.

"I can't believe Fritz is here. You must be over the moon," Krystal said, her voice filled with excitement.

"*Jah*, all that worrying was for nothing!" Wilma chimed in.

"I know. It seems unreal."

"But why did he bring Peter along?" Krystal asked.

"Talk about a tense evening," Ada muttered under her breath.

"Peter is his brother. He's bound to be in our lives. Peter was good to me and Jared for a long time."

"That's a good way to view things, Debbie," Wilma responded while wiping down the counter. "Family ties matter. It's always better if everyone gets along."

Debbie nodded, biting her lip. She thought Peter would keep his distance once Fritz moved to be with her. She didn't express her feelings to the others, but she felt uneasy with Peter around, considering what he'd done in the past.

"Did you set a date for the wedding?" Krystal asked, passing her a plate to dry.

"Not yet. I didn't want to push him tonight."

"You can ask him tomorrow," Ada suggested as she neatly stacked the dishes by the sink.

"And find out what his favorite cakes are, too," Wilma added.

Debbie smiled. "I will."

"It's a perfect time for him to be here, just when we're discussing cakes," Ada pointed out. "We can bake more tomorrow, Wilma. All our samples are gone now."

"Ah, yes. We'll do that."

"Yay! I love cakes." Jared clapped his hands.

Debbie looked over at her son. "Time for bed, Jared."

"Aww, do I have to?"

"Yes, it's past your bedtime." Debbie set the tea towel aside, ready to accompany him to his room.

Jared raised his hand. "I can go to my room on my own, *Mamm*."

Laughter echoed around the kitchen as Jared left the room.

"And remember, no more sneaking out or disappearing, okay?" Debbie called after him.

"I'm just going to my room," Jared's voice faded away as he climbed the stairs.

CHAPTER 14

*W*ilma cherished the tranquil mornings at the orchard. At times, she would go for a peaceful walk through the trees after everyone had left the house and before Ada's arrival. But today was laundry day, and her stroll would have to wait.

Wilma was busily hanging out the laundry as the sun gradually warmed the day. An unexpected cool breeze swept past her, making her wish she had worn a coat before stepping outside.

She wondered how Matthew was coping, spending nights on the porch. So far, it seemed like everyone was doing well with ignoring him. No doubt, he'd expected loads of attention with his stunt.

Despite everything, Wilma was relieved to see that Matthew was still committed to his work. His issues with Krystal seemed not to affect his professional life, at least as far as she could tell.

Just as she was nearly finished hanging out the washing, something out of the corner of her eye caught her attention.

She glanced up to find the stray orange dog observing her from a short distance. She'd seen it before, and no one had been able to find it since. Startled, she leaped back. "Shoo!"

The dog didn't budge but simply continued to stare at her.

Gaining a bit more courage, Wilma talked to the dog, "What are you staring at? Never seen anyone hang laundry before?"

In response, the dog wagged its tail. Wilma recalled Krystal's worry about the dog possibly being hungry, and Wilma hated the thought of any creature suffering.

"Hold on there. I'll be right back." Wilma quickly gathered the laundry basket and retreated inside. She took the leftover bacon from breakfast and tossed it to the dog. The way the animal quickly devoured the food confirmed her suspicion that it was indeed a stray, and a famished one at that.

Still uncertain about her next move, Wilma heard her name being called. She spun around to see Eli and Obadiah approaching. Being at the back of the house, she hadn't heard them arrive.

A sigh of relief escaped her lips. As they neared, they noticed the dog by her side. Obadiah, looking concerned, asked, "Wilma, are you alright?"

"Yes, I'm fine. It's a rather delightful little dog."

"Not so little," Obadiah remarked.

"Is this the stray you spotted the other day?" Eli inquired.

"Yes. Fairfax was on the lookout for him but couldn't find him. It seems he's taken a liking to me."

"He must sense you're an animal lover," Obadiah stated, a smile playing on his lips. "We should keep our distance for now. It would be best to get him checked by a vet to ensure he's not carrying any diseases or rabies. Good thing I left my dog at home today," Obadiah said.

"I gave him some bacon, and he gulped it down," Wilma shared.

"Ah, poor fellow!" Obadiah cooed, approaching the dog cautiously. "Come here, buddy."

"I could get him more food. He seems to be starving," Wilma suggested.

"That's a good idea," Eli agreed.

Without any further delay, Wilma dashed inside the house, returning with some chicken she had scraped off leftover bones from the previous night's dinner. She passed the plate to Obadiah.

"Thank you, Wilma," Obadiah beamed, their hands grazing lightly during the exchange and sparking a blush on Wilma's cheeks.

As soon as the dog caught a whiff of the food, he energetically ran toward Obadiah, waiting patiently at his feet. "Good boy," he praised, placing the dish on the ground and watching as the dog demolished the meal almost instantly. Then, he improvised a leash using his suspenders and fastened it around the dog's neck.

"Good thinking!" Wilma complimented.

"We'll get him to the vet right away," Obadiah assured her, glancing up for confirmation. "That's alright with you, Wilma?"

"Absolutely. Just be cautious. He might bite."

"He seems well-behaved. We'll return with updates," Obadiah added.

"Yes, please keep me posted about our little friend," Wilma requested, a bit embarrassed by her show of concern, but it seemed to charm Obadiah, who rewarded her with a wide grin.

Once the men had left, Wilma busied herself with tidying the house. After a while, she took a break and prepared a pot of tea and sandwiches, anticipating Ada's arrival.

With the weather becoming more pleasant, she enjoyed her morning tea outdoors on the porch. As she settled the tray on the table between the chairs, her gaze drifted to Matthew's makeshift camp.

Her brow furrowed as she noticed the small tent that had seemingly sprung up out of nowhere. How could she have missed that?

Intrigued, she ventured closer and peeped inside. A gas stove with a saucepan on top, a standing flashlight at the back, and neatly folded clothes in one corner greeted her. Shaking her head in disbelief, Wilma couldn't help but think that Matthew was planning for a prolonged stay.

Samuel and Ada arrived just as Wilma settled into her seat. Ada raised her hand in farewell to Samuel, then ascended the porch steps.

"Great timing," Wilma observed, gesturing toward the pot of steaming tea.

"*Wunderbaar.* I trust the tea is still hot?"

"Freshly poured," Wilma confirmed with a nod, and Ada sank down next to her, placing a shopping bag by her feet. Wilma subtly tilted her head toward Matthew's pile of belongings, catching Ada's attention. "Notice anything unusual?"

Ada squinted, her gaze landing on Matthew's temporary shelter. "What is that collection of things?"

"That," Wilma replied with a heavy sigh, "is Matthew's entire world right now."

Ada shook her head, her lips forming a tight line. "He really needs to let go. Matthew is just embarrassing himself now."

Wilma frowned, her fingers drumming on the table's surface. "So, we just ignore him?"

Ada nodded firmly. "It's for the best."

Wilma looked down at Ada's shopping bag. "What's in there?"

"Flour," Ada replied.

"But we already have so much," Wilma pointed out.

Ada paused mid-motion of reaching for her tea, her eyes fixed on Wilma. "You haven't noticed Susan's cake consumption, have you? It's practically a feat. I don't want to be caught off guard on our next baking day."

Wilma chuckled, shaking her head. "Alright, Ada. Now, there's something else I need to share." Leaning in closer, Wilma retold her encounter with the stray dog.

CHAPTER 15

*a*s Simon and Melvin eagerly welcomed Zeke to discuss alpacas that same afternoon, the homely kitchen saw Harriet and Favor bustling about, preparing lunch. The harmonious hum of Harriet's tune filled the air as Favor contended with a flurry of unsettling thoughts beside her.

Anxiety gripped Favor, her head spun, and her thoughts grew louder, drowning Harriet's humming. The onslaught of sensations was overwhelming. Suddenly, Favor's stomach clenched, and she retched unexpectedly on the kitchen floor.

Harriet's knife clattered to the cutting board as she rushed to Favor's side, promptly securing her *kapp* strings away from the mess.

"I'm fine," Favor insisted, dabbing at her face with the corner of her apron.

"No, you're not," Harriet firmly contradicted. "You need rest."

Favor found herself being led to her room without the strength to protest. She was too drained to even worry about the unkempt state of her room – the bed unmade, Simon's shoes strewn around, and her nightgown casually draped over a chair.

Tucked under the covers, Favor felt Harriet's cool hand on her forehead, checking for fever while seemingly ignoring the disorder around them.

"Rest. I'll make some soothing mint tea. You're not to leave this bed," Harriet instructed.

"Harriet, please don't worry. A few minutes rest, and I'll be back on my feet." Favor's eyes started closing.

"That's not happening. You need to unwind." And with those final words, Harriet left the room.

Despite closing her eyes, Favor's worries persisted. What if Harriet suspected her of faking illness to evade chores? Her mother-in-law never missed an opportunity to label her lazy.

The rest of the day passed in a blur. Favor drifted between wakefulness and sleep, bouts of sickness interrupting her rest. Through it all, Harriet remained steadfast by her side, mopping her sweaty brow and dutifully refreshing the bucket beside the bed.

When Favor's eyes fluttered open, the soft glow from the lamp told her it was nighttime. Her gaze found Harriet sitting quietly in the corner. Thankfully, the world seemed less shaky, and her stomach a little more settled.

"Where's Simon?" she asked, her voice a hoarse whisper.

Harriet's posture straightened. "How do you feel?"

"Better," Favor admitted.

"Are you certain?"

"Yes, I am. But what time is it? And where's Simon?"

"He's been here throughout the afternoon, but he's now having supper with Melvin. I stayed, just in case you needed anything."

On her bedside table, Favor spotted a tray of food. "Harriet, thank you for caring for me. It seems like a nasty bout of the flu. You shouldn't get too close." Favor pushed herself up into a seated position.

Standing up, Harriet placed the tray gently on Favor's lap. "I've been careful. I've kept my distance."

Favor couldn't help but feel touched. She couldn't remember when she felt so unwell, and Harriet had been so caring.

When Simon finally appeared, Harriet quietly excused herself.

"What happened?" Simon questioned, settling into the bed next to her.

"I'm okay," she assured him.

"I was worried. You were asleep each time I checked in. Could you be pregnant?"

Favor contemplated his words. "Isn't morning sickness, well, restricted to mornings?"

"I'm not sure."

"Neither am I. But wouldn't it be wonderful if I was? A little sickness would be a small price to pay."

"Don't get ahead of yourself. The last thing we need is another disappointment."

"I'll contact the doctor tomorrow. Some of the tests should be back."

"That's right, you went to the doctor," he murmured, his words hanging in the air.

"They had just received a cancelation when I got there."

"God is watching over us," Simon mused.

Favor cast a warm smile at Simon. "Harriet was an incredible help today."

"Both Ma and Pa are quite concerned for you."

"I wonder... if I am pregnant, would it be a boy or a girl? Or maybe even twins. They do run in the family. Earl and Miriam just had their third set of multiples. Christina and Mark have twins too. But maybe just one would be best to start until I get the hang of this parenting thing. It's better to make one mistake at a time rather than multiple."

Simon chuckled. "You're not going to mess up. And we'll manage, no matter what. But let's remember this might not be the right time yet."

Favor's eyes sparkled with excitement. "I would love a little girl. I've mostly been around girls."

"I understand." Simon nodded. "I'm sorry again for my folks being here. I know it's the last thing you want."

Exhaling a heavy sigh, Favor responded, "I can't say I'm pleased about it. It feels like we'll never have a moment alone unless we're secluded like this. That's been our reality so far, and it doesn't look like it's about to change."

"Don't say that. We came here to be by ourselves, and it'll happen. Just believe it."

"Thank you." Favor returned his smile even though she wasn't at all confident about what he said.

CHAPTER 16

*K*rystal couldn't find anyone to work in her store. Everyone who normally filled in for her at the quilt store was unavailable, so she asked Jed to spend the day with her. Naturally, she put him to work.

Krystal leaned against the doorframe of the backroom, watching him scrub the small sink.

He looked at her and smiled. "You know, I could get used to this."

"Cleaning?"

He chuckled. "No. Being with you all day, every day."

"Well, don't get used to it. This store only needs one person. You have to get busy starting our tour guide business. This is going to work out perfectly."

"Samuel and I were up late last night talking about

it. He's going to help. He's got a wagon I can use, and he knows where I can get two draft horses to pull it. Samuel said the owner might even allow me to pay them off over time."

She straightened up. "That's great news. Why didn't you tell me?"

"I'm telling you now."

Krystal smiled. "I'm glad you've already made a start. It's important to have something that you're passionate about."

Jed nodded. "Yeah, I'm excited about it. But I must admit, I will miss spending time with you throughout the day."

Krystal walked over to him and placed a hand on his arm. "I'll miss you too, Jed."

He turned toward her. They both stood there in silence for a moment, lost in each other's eyes.

Then Jed turned away. "I'm not getting much work done. There's a coffee shop near here, isn't there?"

Krystal giggled. "I think you're trying to get out of cleaning. You keep taking breaks. You can't do that when you're taking people on a tour."

Jed chuckled. "I guess. You're something else, Krystal."

"What can I say? You bring out the best in me."

Jed's eyes wandered down to Krystal's lips before he looked back up at her eyes. "You know, we could take a break right now. Maybe go for a walk or something."

"No. I'd have to close my store."

"Put a sign up that you're closed for lunch."

"No." Krystal laughed. "I'll do no such thing. I need every sale I can get. People won't come back if I'm closed all the time."

Jed nodded, his face falling slightly. "Right, of course. I understand."

Krystal could sense his disappointment and didn't want him to feel rejected. She walked over to him and touched his chest, feeling his heart beating rapidly. "But... we could have lunch together. Right here, in the back room."

Jed's eyes lit up, and he grinned. "I like the sound of that."

When midday rolled around, they sat together in the small backroom.

They chatted about the tour business as they ate the sandwiches Krystal had brought from home. But their conversation gradually shifted to more personal topics, and they found themselves opening up to each other in ways they never had before.

Krystal talked some more about her difficult childhood and how she had worked hard to create a successful business on her own. Jed listened attentively, his eyes never leaving hers as he reached out to take her hand in his.

"You've been through so much, Krystal. It's made you so strong."

Krystal felt her cheeks flush at his words and the touch of his hand. "Thanks, Jed. I've had to overcome a lot. I think I keep improving and becoming a better person. I hope I am, anyway."

Jed leaned in, his hand brushing a stray strand of hair from her face. "Well, you don't have to be strong all the time. You can let someone else take care of you for a change."

Krystal felt her heart skip a beat as she gazed into his eyes. "I will allow you to take care of me."

"We'll marry as soon as I can support us."

"I can't wait. Now get back to work." She stood up and put their plates in the sink.

He chuckled. "All right, boss."

The front doorbell sounded as a customer came through the door. "Oh, a customer," she whispered.

"Sell a lot," he whispered back. "We'll need the money."

Krystal greeted the customer, leaving Jed to wash the plates.

While assisting the customer, Krystal's mind kept straying to the shared future she and Jed had recently discussed. Transforming their dreams into reality would require substantial effort, yet she knew that they could make it happen by relying on God.

When the customer left, Krystal returned to the backroom to find Jed sitting on a stool, lost in thought. She walked up to him and placed a hand on his shoulder. "Hey, what's wrong?"

He turned to look at her, a serious expression on his face. "Krystal, there's something I need to tell you."

Krystal's heart skipped a beat. "What is it?"

Jed took a deep breath. "I know we just talked about getting married and starting a life together, but there's something I need to tell you before we take any further steps."

Krystal's heart sank as she listened to Jed. She felt she knew what was coming, but she couldn't help the disappointment that flooded her. She took a step back, looking at him with sad eyes.

"What is it, Jed?" she asked softly. Now she was worried. Has he married already? Had he fathered a child out of wedlock? Perhaps... both?

"It's something I was told in confidence, and I'm not sure if I should say something, but I don't like having secrets from you."

"You better tell me. I'm worried now."

"Okay. It's about my brother, Malachi."

Krystal was relieved that his worry was about someone else. She sank into a chair. "Go on."

"It's about the land that Favor and Simon bought along with the other young couples."

"What does that have to do with Malachi?"

"It was his land that he divided up. He doesn't want people to know how rich he is."

Krystal's mind ticked over. "He's wealthy?"

"Yes. I'm telling you this because there is one block of land left. It's going cheap. We could buy it, which would be a great start. Favor is your best friend, and you'd live next door."

Krystal breathed out heavily. "I had no idea it was Malachi's land."

"Yeah, well, don't tell anyone. Only my uncle knows, and Cherish would know too, but they are all keeping quiet."

"I won't say a thing to anyone," Krystal assured him.

"I wanted to throw that information out there before I start this tour business just in case you want to move there and make a fresh start. I'll find the money for the land somehow."

"It would be a great start for us, but I couldn't leave my quilt store. I can't move the store there either because there wouldn't be many customers in Willersburg. All my friends are here too, and Wilma is like a mother to me."

"I thought about that, but you'll have Favor and Cherish. And don't you sell online as well? If your bishop has given you permission, the bishop in Willersburg will also give you permission. I'm sure of it."

"No, I get tour busses coming here full of tourists. They spend a lot of money. I wouldn't get that many customers if I moved."

Jed rubbed his chin. "Did you say the tourists come in buses?"

"Yes."

He rubbed his chin. "I like the sound of that."

Krystal wasn't sure what he meant, but she hoped he realized she wasn't moving anywhere. She'd told him often enough.

CHAPTER 17

*A*t Ada and Samuel's house the next day, Jed worked hard on his new business venture. Samuel had taken Ada to the orchard before returning to help fix up the old wagon.

Samuel had said that it would look as good as new with a bit of paint and grease. Jed wasn't so sure. He thought there might be a better way.

Jed finished up his repairs, wiped off his hands with a cloth, and threw the cloth over his shoulder as he stood beside the wagon while Samuel polished the rims.

Jed had developed a fondness for Ada and Samuel and was grateful to them for taking him in. He expected Ada's abrasive exterior masked a heart of gold. If he was wrong, at the very least, she kept him entertained. Similarly, he appreciated the occasional profound word spoken by Samuel.

"Thanks for all your help, Samuel."

"My pleasure. We're making good progress on the wagon. Have you been giving any thought to how to get the word out?"

"Excuse me?"

"How you'll let people know about the tours. You won't get anywhere if no one knows about it. You'll also have to organize the destinations."

"Yes, I've been giving everything some thought. The only thing is..."

Samuel looked up at him. "What's that?"

"The wagon can only accommodate a few people at a time. If we had a bus, we could fit three times as many passengers and make three times more money."

Samuel scratched his beard. "A horse-drawn bus?"

Jed burst out laughing. "No. A regular bus."

Samuel's mouth twisted to one side as he stared at Jed. "And who would drive the bus?"

Jed pulled back his shoulders, grinning. "Me."

Samuel stared at Jed in disbelief. "You want to drive a bus?"

"I will if the bishop gives me permission," Jed responded. "I reckon it's the perfect solution."

Samuel thought for a moment. "There's no way he'd give you permission. It's not going to happen."

Jed shrugged his shoulders. "I've lived in other communities where the bishop allows tractors for business purposes. A bus and a tractor are pretty closely related, I'd reckon."

Samuel removed his hat and wiped the beads of sweat from his forehead. "I think you're way off there. A tractor is farming equipment used to produce more food, which is understandable. A bus is something different."

Jed was convinced he could talk the bishop into it. He was good with people, and they generally did whatever he asked. "It depends on how you look at it. I mean, I'd only drive for my job when I'm giving the tours."

Samuel sighed. "Best if you speak to the bishop before you do anything. I'm certain the answer will be no. It's not how we do things in this community."

Jed stayed silent, not mentioning that he had already arranged to look at a local bus for sale. He worked on the wagon for a few more moments before saying, "I forgot I had an appointment. I'll take a break and head into town. Do you need anything while I'm there?"

Samuel shook his head. "No. Would you like me to come with you?"

"No, that's all right," Jed said as he dusted off his hands. "Can I borrow a buggy?"

"Sure. Help yourself. Take the buggy I was driving this morning and Jack, the horse with the long white socks."

"Thanks, Samuel." Jed gave Samuel a nod and then set off.

When Jed arrived at the car yard, he saw a bus

parked near the road. It was an older model than he'd expected, but the paintwork appeared in good condition. If it drove all right, he'd have it looked over by a mechanic before they discussed the price.

He walked over and saw a middle-aged man sitting in a building in the car lot. The man stood. "Hi there. The name's Ronald. How can I help you?"

"Hi, Ronald. I'm Jed. I spoke to you earlier about the bus."

"That's right." They shook hands, and then Ronald looked over at the bus. "She's a beauty, ain't she?" Before Jed could speak, Ronald added, "I'll grab the keys, and you can take her for a test drive. You got a license, don't you?"

Jed had no driver's license. He'd also taught himself to drive. "Not exactly. Not on me."

"I'll take your word for it." Ronald grabbed a key from a board of keys and handed it to Jed.

"Thank you."

"I'll run you through a few things." They headed through the rows of cars until they came to the bus.

Ronald showed him how to open and close the doors and how to adjust the seat and the mirrors. "Now you're set to go."

"Good. Are you coming with me?"

"No. I've got to watch the yard, but if you don't return, I'll keep that." Ronald pointed to the horse and buggy.

Jed smiled and didn't reveal that it wasn't even his horse and buggy.

When the man moved away, Jed buckled his seat belt, turned the key, and the engine rumbled to life.

He moved onto the road and drove along the streets effortlessly. He was impressed at how it turned the corners and maneuvered in and around cars.

He had imagined himself doing this daily; talking to the passengers, providing them with details of what they were seeing, and making a joke or two for a pleasant atmosphere.

Jed checked the rear-view mirrors as he was heading back, feeling quite optimistic. But when he looked back at the road, someone was standing in the way! He immediately hit the brakes. The bus lurched to a halt just in front of the man.

Jed rushed out to make sure he was alright. And then he realized who it was.

Matthew stood there, surprised and scared. When Matthew saw him, his face turned red with fury as he stared at Jed and the bus. "Are you okay?" Jed asked.

"You tried to kill me."

"No, I didn't. I didn't see you."

"What are you doing driving a bus?" Matthew's voice rose.

"Testing it for our new business," Jed answered.

"What business is that?" Matthew snapped.

"Tours of the orchard and other attractions. Forget about that. Are you sure you're okay?" Jed asked again.

Matthew pushed past him, bumping his shoulder as he walked away. "I'm still alive. Sorry to disappoint you," he mumbled without turning back.

Jed was in no mood to drive now. He returned to the car yard and handed back the key, telling the salesman he'd think about it.

Then he went to Krystal's store to say hello while he was in town.

She was busy serving a customer when he arrived, so he waited patiently until she was finished.

Then he walked behind the counter and pulled her into a deep hug. Krystal smiled. "What's this for?"

"Do I need a reason to hug my future wife?" he asked, his tone light and teasing.

"No, I suppose not."

He stepped away from her and leaned against the counter. "How has your day been?"

"It's been busy today. How about you? How is the wagon coming along?"

He was about to tell her about his bus idea when someone burst through the door. Krystal jumped in shock, and both she and Jed turned to see Matthew.

"Matthew, what are you doing here?" Krystal asked.

With his eyes set on Jed, he backed away. "Nothing important," he muttered as he shook his head at Jed and turned around, and walked out the door.

Krystal scowled before turning back to Jed. "I'm sorry for his behavior. I don't understand what his problem is."

Jed hadn't planned on telling Krystal what had happened. He knew she was already upset with Matthew and what he was doing. The last thing he wanted was to stress Krystal further.

But then he considered it was better to tell her what happened than for her to hear it from Matthew.

"I think I know why he's so mad," Jed began as Krystal knit her brow in confusion.

"Why?"

"Today, I was test-driving a bus for the tours."

Krystal blinked. "A bus?"

He could tell by her tone that she wasn't pleased. "With a bus, we could take more people on the tour and make more money."

She silently nodded as if it were no big deal. Jed was relieved at how Krystal received this news until he remembered she wasn't raised Amish. It was normal for people to drive buses and cars where she came from.

"Everything seemed to be going alright until Matthew crossed the street without looking."

Krystal's eyes widened in surprise. "What do you mean?"

"I didn't hit him. It was close, but the brakes on the bus were good. I got out to check if he was alright, and he was really mad."

Krystal bit her lip. "Let me get this straight. You were driving a bus, and you nearly ran over Matthew?"

"Correct. Why was he even in town? Doesn't he work at the orchard or something?"

Krystal nodded. "Maybe this all happened for a reason: to wake him up."

"Could be," Jed replied with a shrug.

"Thanks for letting me know, but I doubt the bishop will allow you to drive a bus. And please don't do anything without asking permission from the bishop first. If other people see you, it won't reflect well on us. If you want to stay in this—"

"I know. You're right. I should have asked first, but I didn't think there would be any harm if I couldn't drive it anyway—so there was no point in asking the bishop in the first place until I found that out."

"I guess that makes sense," Krystal said, trying to sound calm, although inside, she was worried about who else might have seen him driving the bus. "Please let this be the last time you go against the rules."

"I assure you it will. I kind of didn't see it as breaking any rules."

"It was. I just want to live in peace and do the right thing."

He nodded. "You can rely on me. I won't disappoint you."

She looked into his eyes and believed him.

CHAPTER 18

*M*atthew was seething with rage. He couldn't stand Jed starting a business at the orchard when he felt like it should have been him.

After years of hard work toiling in the orchard, he felt he deserved a promotion of some sort. Yes, that would impress Krystal.

He marched over to Fairfax's house, hoping to talk with him and find out about any future career prospects. When he got closer, he noticed Fairfax in the barn.

Fairfax looked up. "Matthew, where have you been?"

Matthew could tell from Fairfax's voice that he was not pleased.

"I had to take care of some business downtown. I wanted to ask you something."

Fairfax's eyebrows drew together. "Your job is here, not in town. Did you go to see Krystal again?"

"Yes. I saw her briefly."

"You'll have to make up the time, and please don't disappear again. We're getting so busy now with harvest approaching."

"Sorry." Fairfax continued working while Matthew talked. "Am I ever going to get a promotion at the orchard, or do I have to stay a farmhand forever?"

Fairfax stopped what he was doing and pushed his hat back on his head. "You can't be serious."

"I am. I've got high hopes of getting my own place one day."

"Well, firstly, you must start taking your work more seriously before that can happen. And if you want to hear what I think, you're closer to losing your job than getting any sort of promotion."

"I've always taken my work seriously."

"You were an able employee, but you've become lazy. If you dedicated yourself to apple trees with the same enthusiasm that you pursue Krystal, you'd be an expert by now."

Fairfax's words had a strong impact on Matthew. He had to do better.

"Listen, we need to focus on the harvest that's coming up. If you put your mind to it, I could give you more responsibility."

The spark in Matthew's eyes was visible. "Like what?"

"You could manage the workers coming for the harvest season. Or since Florence can't do it this year, you could take charge of leading tours of the orchard with the local English schoolchildren."

Matthew pondered on that idea. If Krystal witnessed him acting as a leader and facilitator to the school kids, she would surely be impressed. And if the tours with the children conflicted with what Jed was doing, all the better.

"Thanks, Fairfax. I am grateful for this opportunity. I'd love to take over both of those things. My lazy days are behind me. I'll step up to whatever you give me. I'd love to show the children around."

"No problem," Fairfax said. "Now, I need you to get back to work."

"Sure thing." Matthew went back to work with renewed hope.

WHEN CHERISH WOKE, she rose from the bed and glanced out the window. The first sight that greeted her was Malachi heading to the barn, accompanied by Caramel and Wally by his side.

She quickly got dressed, ran a brush through her hair, and then put on her prayer *kapp*, carefully tucking her hair underneath. Once fully dressed, Cherish made her way to the kitchen.

Opening the gas-powered refrigerator, she retrieved

some eggs and bacon for breakfast. Cherish enjoyed maintaining a clean house and caring for Malachi and their animals. As she heard the back door open, she set the food on the table, readying herself to welcome Malachi as he entered the room.

"Perfect timing!" she said.

Malachi offered a small smile, seeming distracted. Wally and Caramel followed behind him. Caramel headed straight for his bed, but Wally stayed glued to Malachi's side.

"I'm afraid there might be something wrong with Wally," Malachi said.

"What do you mean? What happened?"

Malachi shrugged. "I'm not sure, but he won't leave my side."

"He's always like that."

"More so than usual, though. Look, he won't go to his bed." Malachi tried to usher Wally to his bed, but it was useless. He stayed close and refused to go anywhere near his bed.

Cherish frowned. "He'll be fine. He's probably just sensing some changes."

"I have been gone a lot lately helping with Simon and Favor's house."

"That's probably all it is."

They both closed their eyes and said a silent prayer of thanks for their food.

As they started to eat, Cherish said, "I was thinking

of checking up on Favor and Simon. I want to see how Favor's getting on with Simon's parents."

"I'll come with you."

"Okay. We won't stay long." Cherish screwed up her face. "I feel bad for Favor. She was pleased to be free. Who would have expected them to just show up like that?"

"You didn't think it was possible? I thought it was bound to happen," Malachi said between mouthfuls of food.

Cherish loaded some eggs onto her fork. "It seems Harriet has always done what she wants. No one has ever stopped her. I think it's unfair on Favor if she has to be the one to say anything."

Malachi looked up from his food. "Wait. You don't want me to say something, do you?"

Cherish laughed. "Of course not. That would be worse. No. I think Simon should've said something a long time ago, but he never did, and now Harriet is totally out of control. Favor even said they could move here, but it was supposed to happen in a few years, not a day after they finally moved into their house."

"Don't worry so much. We'll have to help Simon's folks find a place."

"That would be good. We could ask at the general store. Sam might know of something."

"Good idea."

CHAPTER 19

Favor lay in bed, her body weakened by illness. The room felt suffocating as anxiety swirled around her. She mustered the strength to turn her head toward Simon, her voice barely above a whisper. "Please call the doctor and ask for the results of the tests I've done."

"I don't think they'll tell me," Simon said.

"They will. I said you might be the one calling."

"You did?"

"Yes."

He grinned. "You think of everything."

"I hope I'm pregnant. If I'm not, I'll be worried about what's wrong with me."

Simon's eyes widened with a mixture of excitement and concern. He reached out to hold Favor's hand. "I'll go now."

"Okay. Hurry."

Leaving Favor's side, Simon quietly slipped out of the room, careful not to disturb his parents. He made his way to Zeke's barn, where they had a phone.

In the dimly lit barn, Simon found Zeke tending to the alpacas. Zeke looked up, surprised. "Hi, Simon."

Simon took a deep breath, his voice hushed. "I need to use your phone, if that's all right."

Concern etched into Zeke's features as he led Simon to the corner of the barn where the phone was mounted on the wall. "Of course, Simon. Take your time. When you're finished, I'll tell you about a place that might be coming up for lease."

"Great."

Zeke walked out and left him alone.

With trembling hands, Simon dialed the doctor's number. As he waited for the call to connect, a mix of hope and fear coursed through his veins. Every passing second felt like an eternity.

Finally, he got through to the doctor and he asked for Favor's results.

There was a brief silence on the other end of the line as if the doctor was carefully considering his response. Simon's breath hitched, his heart pounding in his chest.

"I have the results right here," the doctor finally replied. "I'm pleased to inform you that Favor's test results came back positive. She's pregnant."

A surge of joy washed over Simon, overwhelming him with emotion. His eyes glistened with tears of happiness. "Thank you, Doctor. Thank you so much. This is incredible news."

"Congratulations."

"Is it for sure?" Simon asked.

"Absolutely."

Simon rubbed his beard. "She's been sick."

"Most likely morning sickness. It will pass."

"Thanks again."

"She should come in for another check-up in a few weeks."

"I'll see that she does. Although, we use midwives."

"Very well."

"But I don't know if there's one around here," Simon said. "We've only just moved here, you see."

"We can talk about that later."

"Thanks again." Simon ended the call and took a moment to collect his thoughts. He was going to be a father. Tears stung at the back of his eyes. He couldn't wait to share the life-changing news with Favor. They'd both been waiting for this for years.

Simon then found Zeke and heard about a possible place for his parents to stay. Everything was falling into place.

Returning to Favor's bedside, Simon's face beamed with a smile he could hardly contain.

She looked over at him when he walked into the room. He sat on the bed beside her. "We did it. You're pregnant. We're going to have a baby."

Favor's eyes widened with joy, her pale face lighting

up. She reached out for Simon's hand, tears of happiness welling in her eyes. For a moment, she couldn't speak. "Don't joke with me. Because if you are, it's not funny."

He shook his head. "I'd never joke about anything like that. The doctor said it's for sure. It's for real. You're pregnant, one hundred percent."

Favor touched her stomach. "A baby," she murmured before she looked back at Simon. "We're having a baby."

"We are," Simon said softly.

Favor shook her head. "We can't tell anyone yet."

"No one?" he asked.

Favor's mouth fell open. "You didn't, did you?"

"No," he whispered, "I haven't told anyone."

"We have to wait a few months."

He grinned. "It's the best secret I'll ever keep."

"Me too."

He leaned over and kissed her forehead.

"*Mamm* will be so excited and your mother too," Favor said.

"I know."

CHAPTER 20

s the late morning sun hung in the sky, Cherish and Malachi found themselves on the doorstep of Favor and Simon's home. Their visit to the general store had been fruitless, leaving them without any leads for leasing opportunities.

Wally, who remained stubbornly attached to Malachi, was part of their entourage. Similarly, Caramel had tagged along since leaving him at home wasn't an option. If they were taking one pet, they had to take the other. However, Caramel seemed content to snooze in the buggy.

Before they could knock, Harriet swung the door open, greeting them with surprise. "Cherish! Malachi! What a pleasant surprise this morning."

"Hello, Harriet," Cherish responded.

"And you've brought your little duck." Harriet stared at their pet.

"He's a goose," Cherish clarified.

"Ah, of course," Harriet responded, although her gaze fixed on Wally. "Does he usually come indoors?"

Malachi said, "We think he's not feeling well and refuses to leave my side. But don't worry. He's pretty well house-trained."

"Simon and Favor won't mind him in the house," Cherish assured her.

Harriet raised a questioning eyebrow but reluctantly stepped aside, allowing them in. "Just in time for breakfast. Come this way."

"Thanks, but we've already had breakfast."

Harriet looked at Malachi. "Men are always hungry. You can eat again can't you, Malachi?"

"I guess so."

"And look at you, Cherish, skinny as a rake. We need to fatten you up. Follow me."

Malachi and Cherish exchanged smiles as they followed Harriet to the kitchen. Simon and Melvin were already seated at the table.

"Hey there, you two!" Simon's cheerful voice filled the room. "And hello, Wally."

"Morning," Malachi responded as he and Cherish sat at the table.

"Did I hear you say Wally's sick?" Simon inquired, his eyes filled with genuine concern.

Malachi glanced at his feathered companion. "Maybe. He's a bit more clingy than usual."

Cherish's attention shifted to the delicious spread of

eggs, cornmeal mush, and pancakes. "Harriet, everything looks wonderful. And there's maple syrup too, my favorite."

Malachi nodded in agreement. "It all looks amazing."

"Help yourselves, there's plenty for all," Harriet offered.

Cherish scanned the room as she forked a piece of pancake. She'd only just eaten, but everything looked too good to pass up. "Is Favor still catching up on sleep?" she inquired, noticing her sister's absence.

"Yes, she's not feeling very well today," Harriet said.

"Really?"

"Ma stayed up all night taking care of her. She was wonderful."

"Nonsense!" Harriet dismissed Simon's comment with a wave of her hand.

"I got some sleep. That new bed is like sleeping on a cloud. Thank you for being so generous, Malachi and Cherish."

Cherish didn't know what to say. She wasn't used to Harriet being nice and not complaining. The bed was just an average bed.

Simon continued, "Ma told me to leave the room so she could take care of Favor properly. She was with her most of the night."

Cherish looked over at Harriet. "That was good of you."

"I only did what needed to be done."

"On another note, I think I found a place that might be available to lease soon," Simon said, swiftly changing the topic.

"Where's the property located?" Malachi asked as he cut a piece of bacon.

"It's just down the road. It's not available yet, but Zeke heard about it from a friend."

Melvin gave a slight nod as he stirred his cornmeal mush. "We'll check it out. If it's not awful, we'll take it."

Cherish was relieved to hear it. "How has the transition been for you two? You must miss your farm."

"We don't care where we are as long as we're close to Simon." Harriet's face beamed.

"Simon and Favor have been so kind that it almost feels like home here—our second home," Melvin said.

"I've been savoring time with my Simon these past few days. Of course, I'll look forward to extending such delightfulness to Favor when she recovers."

"Have you got any new ideas about what to do with the land yet?" Malachi asked Simon.

"We've been discussing alpacas with Zeke, learning more about them," Simon replied.

"That seems like a good direction for us to go," Melvin stated as if he and Harriet planned to live together with Simon and Favor. "I wasn't sure at first, but Zeke is confident. What he said about the animals made sense. I think we might make a success of it."

There was a lull in the conversation, and Cherish finished her pancake. "I'll check on Favor."

"No, don't. She's still sleeping," Harriet replied.

Cherish was less than thrilled. If Favor was still asleep, she would never have disturbed her. Furthermore, Favor was her sister, whereas Harriet was just Favor's mother-in-law. But to maintain harmony, Cherish had to go along with Harriet, who appeared to have taken over the household. "Alright, I'll wait a bit longer," Cherish said.

Several moments later, Harriet stood. "I think it's time to see how Favor is. Would you like to come with me, Cherish?"

"Certainly." Cherish found it peculiar to be invited to visit her own sister.

CHAPTER 21

They found her still asleep as they gently pushed open the door to Favor's room. But at their intrusion, her eyes fluttered open.

Slowly sitting up and rubbing her eyes, Favor looked surprised to see Cherish and Harriet by her bedside.

"How do you feel today?" Harriet asked, placing the back of her hand on Favor's forehead in a matronly gesture.

"I'm okay," Favor croaked out, despite her paleness indicating the opposite.

"What's wrong with you?" Cherish asked.

Then, Simon entered the room, announcing, "I think she might've had some spoiled fish."

Favor swiftly brought a hand to her mouth as if on cue, retching into the bucket placed conveniently next to her bed.

"Simon!" Harriet jabbed a finger at him accusingly.

"Don't you know that's the last thing you should say to someone with a bad stomach! Out you get. Go on!"

Simon backed away, and Harriet closed the door on him.

Harriet then hurried back to Favor and took the bucket away from her. "All finished?"

Favor nodded.

"I'll be back in a minute." Harriet hurried away with the bucket to empty it.

When they were alone, Cherish sat on the bed, asking again what was wrong.

"I don't know. I seem to be afflicted with this strange illness. Please stay away from me. I don't want you to get ill too."

Cherish eyed Favor suspiciously. "You never get sick. I can't remember the last time you were ill."

"I know. I guess it's the stress caused by this sudden visit." She tried hard not to meet Cherish's gaze but could feel her sister's eyes burning into her.

"Are you pregnant?" Cherish asked bluntly.

"Shhh," Favor hushed her.

"You are!" Cherish whisper-shouted. "Tell me."

"Yes. I just found out. I had tests done the other day." Favor lunged forward and grabbed Cherish's arm. "I've never been more sick in my life. I wish someone had told me what to expect. This is awful."

Cherish wanted to shout, but she couldn't. She leaned over and hugged her. "I'm so happy. When is the baby due?"

"I've worked it out roughly to March next year. It's only early days. But keep it between us for now, please? Simon and I don't want anyone to know yet. It's official, though."

"Can I tell Malachi? It's so hard to keep things from him."

"Okay, but only if he won't tell anyone."

"He won't. He wouldn't." Cherish couldn't keep the smile from her face. "I imagine Harriet would be suspicious of you being sick and all."

Favor shrugged. "I don't know, but I'm not telling them yet."

"Harriet seems to be taking good care of you."

"It's embarrassing to say, but she's taking care of me way better than Simon ever could've."

"You should think about keeping Harriet around. If you get tired, you can just laze about while Harriet does everything for you."

Favor's lips tilted upward. "Simon said something similar, but I couldn't do that."

"Why not?"

"Hmm. It is tempting. She does everything around here, and she's not so bad, really."

"Is that so?"

"She means well." Favor pulled the quilt higher up.

Cherish could no longer contain her excitement. She hugged Favor again. "This is the best news ever! I'm so excited for you and Simon! And happy for myself."

"Thanks, Cherish, but can you let go? You're kind of squishing me."

Harriet walked back in, and Cherish quickly pulled away from Favor. "Thank you for taking care of her, Harriet. I'm sure with your help, she'll be better in no time."

"Yeah. Thanks, Ma," Favor said.

"It's what mothers are for. I'll get you some mint tea now."

"I don't think I can have anything. Maybe later."

Harriet smiled at Favor and then turned her attention to Cherish. "It might be better if we let your sister rest now."

"Good idea. I'll be back later today." Cherish said goodbye to Favor and walked out of the room, mentally planning out the things she could purchase for the baby.

When Cherish and Malachi arrived home, Cherish made an excuse to go to the store—alone.

When she arrived, she flipped through the catalog choosing wonderful baby things for Favor.

Money was tight for her sister and her brother-in-law, so the least she could do was order them a crib and a few other necessary items.

She'd break the news to Malachi when the goods arrived. Hopefully, he wouldn't mind too much.

Once Cherish placed her orders, she was distracted by the smaller baby items they already had in the store. She couldn't resist getting a few little things.

CHAPTER 22

usan and Daphne arrived at Wilma's house on a bright mid-morning, making it their second visit for the week. Settled comfortably in the living room, they enjoyed hot tea and a little gossip.

"I see Matthew's still hanging around," Daphne remarked, raising her teacup to her lips for a sip.

Wilma affirmed with a nod, "He is."

"Poor guy. Doesn't he have his own place?" Susan asked, a note of sympathy in her voice.

Ada held her tongue, refraining from comment. Whenever Susan wasn't sorry for her words, she seemed to feel sorry for others. Ada decided to keep her thoughts to herself to avoid adding fuel to Susan's perpetual sorrow. "He does have his own home — a cottage in the neighboring orchard."

Susan's brow furrowed in confusion. "Then why is he here?"

Ada gave a shrug. "I can't say for certain. Something about Krystal, I think. He seems to believe that his self-imposed hardship of sleeping on the porch will win her heart. But it only makes sense in his head."

Suppressing a chuckle, Wilma agreed with Ada's assessment.

"I think you ought to charge him rent, Wilma," Daphne proposed.

Wilma couldn't help but grin at the thought. "That's a brilliant idea. Perhaps I will."

With a chuckle, Ada joined in. "Yes, that might encourage him to move along."

"Had we mentioned Fritz arriving the other night?" Wilma asked Susan and Daphne, her memory not as sharp as it once was.

"No! Fritz is here?" Daphne asked with surprise.

"Yes. He showed up with Peter the other night."

"Peter, his brother is back?" Daphne's eyes widened.

"That's rather strange." Susan adjusted her glasses. "Oh! I'm so sorry. I didn't mean to say strange like it was bad."

Ada could no longer keep quiet. "We're all friends here, Susan. You can say whatever comes to mind without being sorry all the time."

"It's alright, Susan. It was very awkward indeed! I have no idea why Peter came with him." Wilma shook her head.

"Maybe he came to see his mother. Peter is courting

someone. We met her. What was her name again, Wilma?"

"I believe it's Maisy."

"That's right."

"That must have been rather uncomfortable for Debbie," Daphne added.

"Yes, well... at least he came back." Ada laughed.

Just then, there was a knock at the door. Ada being the closest one, said that she'd get it. When she opened the door, Ada was startled to find Eli and Obadiah standing there with a large orange dog obediently standing between them.

"Hello. Oh, who is this?" Ada frowned as she looked down at the dog.

"We are here to deliver news about the dog Wilma discovered in the orchard," Obadiah announced.

Knowing Wilma's dislike of dogs, Ada asked the three of them to stay on the porch while she fetched Wilma.

"Wilma, Eli and Obadiah are outside with an unfortunate-looking dog," Ada called out.

Wilma stood up and said to the ladies, "I'll be right back." When Wilma got to the door, Eli and Obadiah stood over Matthew's campsite, studying it closely. The dog was with them.

"It's actually quite an impressive setup," Eli commented.

Obadiah leaned down and opened the lid of the

cooker. "I never knew you could get gas stoves this small."

Then Eli noticed Wilma. "Oh, it's lovely to see you again."

The dog strolled up to Wilma and pushed its nose into her hand, wanting her to pat it.

At first, Wilma recoiled from the dog's touch, but then she remembered Obadiah loved dogs and knew she had to try.

She quickly scratched its head. "Good dog. He looks so different now that he's all cleaned up."

"Wilma, you've allowed Matthew to get even more comfortable here," Eli stated.

"I had no say in it. He just came here and hasn't left. Ada says if we ignore him, he'll realize what he's doing."

"An interesting choice for a campsite. I would have gone for something in the orchard, surrounded by trees," Obadiah said, smiling.

Eli nodded in agreement. "Anyway," Eli went on. "The vet said the dog is healthy! He believes him to be only three or four going by his teeth."

Wilma was surprised. "Oh, I thought he'd be about ten or more."

"Just a bit malnourished, but that's an easy fix." Obadiah smiled at Wilma, and she blushed in response.

"How amazing!" Wilma attempted to sound delighted before she noticed Ada looking skeptical. The dog licked Wilma's fingers, sending shivers up and down her spine.

"Can you find a home for it?" Ada looked up at Eli.

"Wilma will decide. She rescued him." Obadiah moved forward and patted him. "I'd love to have him, but my dog tends to get quite jealous of other dogs."

"Me too. I'd like to take him, but I firmly believe that he'll have a better life running around here in the orchard than at my small house. It's nothing compared to what this land can offer him," Eli said.

"Of course," Wilma replied, trying her best to sound sympathetic to the animal's needs. "But I believe that someone out there would give him a better home than I could. As much as I'd love to keep him, I don't have time to give a dog attention."

"A home with young children would be better, perhaps?" Ada asked, trying to help Wilma out.

"Sometimes dogs choose their owners, not the other way around. I think this dog has chosen you, Wilma." Obadiah smiled broadly.

Wilma looked down at the dog and saw how adoringly the dog was staring up at her. Her heart softened slightly. The dog did need a good home, but it wouldn't be her home.

"I hate to say it, Wilma, but Obadiah might be right."

Wilma looked over at Ada, shocked that she had let her down.

Then she got an idea. She would take the dog

temporarily while she looked for another home. "I guess I could take him until we find his owner."

"What would you like to name him, Wilma?" Obadiah inquired.

Wilma gulped. "Erm..." Wilma had no interest in naming it.

"What about Red?" Ada suggested, sensing the internal battle going on in Wilma's head.

"It's as good a name as any," Wilma agreed.

"Shall we take the dog inside and let it get familiar with its surroundings?" Eli asked.

Wilma's face scrunched in terror. Did she have to bring the dog inside? Ada watched as Wilma's expression shifted. With a smile, Ada replied, "Susan and Daphne are already discussing their weekly gossip in there."

"I hope we aren't interrupting anything," Obadiah said.

"Well..." Wilma hesitated. "I believe Susan is scared of dogs, so it wouldn't be a good time to bring a dog into the house."

Ada raised an eyebrow at her friend. "Maybe it's best if we take him around the back."

"I'll grab some food for him, too," Wilma said.

Once the men had taken Red around the back and given him some food, they left. Ada and Wilma rejoined the ladies.

"Did we hear something about a dog?" Susan asked.

"That's Wilma's new dog, Red," Ada replied.

Daphne was surprised. "You got a dog?"

"Obadiah left it for her," Ada said, flashing a mischievous grin at Wilma, which prompted further questioning from Susan and Daphne.

"That's really kind of him," Susan commented. "Are you two getting along well?"

Wilma felt her blush deepen. "He's nice to everyone," she managed to stammer out.

"He's especially nice to Wilma," Ada added.

"Yes, he gave you a dog," Daphne said, smiling.

"Not really. It was a stray. Wilma found it," Ada told them.

"About the dog," Wilma began. "Would either of you like a lovely dog? He doesn't have rabies."

"No," Daphne and Susan chorused.

CHAPTER 23

*J*ust before Wilma went to bed, she went to the mud room to check on the dog. His eyes were open, and his head was lifted off the rug she had put down for him. "Good boy, I'll see you in the morning," she said softly, then turned off the lamp and went upstairs.

When Wilma lay down on her bed, a movement startled her awake - it was Red! He had gotten comfortable on the end of Wilma's bed without her noticing. She didn't know what to do about it; he seemed harmless, but she worried if she tried to move him, he might bite or growl. Too tired to take him downstairs, Wilma closed her eyes and fell asleep with Red at the foot of her bed.

When the sun shone through the window in the morning, Wilma saw that Red was still there. "Good morning, Red," she said sleepily as he opened his eyes and looked up at her curiously. "It seems we have made a new friendship here!" Red licked his lips as if he had heard something about food. It was comforting to have him there while Wilma tossed and turned during her restless sleep.

The morning light filled the room as she stood up and looked at Red, who was still on the end of her bed. "I guess you're hungry, *jah?*"

The dog just looked at her.

"Let's go make some breakfast."

Wilma walked to the kitchen, and Red followed her. She rummaged through her refrigerator and found some eggs and bacon. She turned to Red and said, "I hope you like your eggs scrambled." Red barked in response and wagged his tail.

As Wilma began to cook, Red sat and watched her every move. She cracked the eggs and began to scramble them in the pan. The aroma of the sizzling bacon filled the room. Red's eyes grew wide with anticipation.

When the eggs and bacon had cooled down, Wilma placed them in a bowl on the floor for Red. He dove right in, gobbling up the food in a matter of seconds. Wilma watched with amusement as Red licked his lips and wagged his tail in satisfaction.

"Don't expect that all the time. It'll mostly be just scraps, okay?"

Red looked up at her with his big, brown eyes as if he understood every word she said. Wilma couldn't help but smile at the dog's innocent expression. It was as if he had been waiting for someone to care for him for a long time.

"I'll find you a good home. I'm sorry I can't keep you, but it just wouldn't work." Wilma walked over to the stove and made herself a cup of coffee. "It's not just you. I don't like any dogs."

Sitting down, sipping the hot liquid, she pondered the dog's situation. She had never wanted a dog, so why did she feel guilty about being unable to keep him?

It was clear that he had bonded with her for some unknown reason, it was flattering in some small way, but it was just a dog!

Red sat patiently at her feet, waiting for her next move. It was as if he knew that she was thinking about him. Wilma sighed deeply and looked down at him. "Do you want to come with me on a walk soon, boy?"

Red barked excitedly and leaped toward the door, wagging his tail frantically.

"We'll do that after breakfast. Don't get too excited, and don't get too attached to me. I don't like you, so remember that."

Wilma knew her words weren't nice, but the dog couldn't understand. He was still staring at her adoringly.

"Don't you get it? I don't like you, so why are you looking at me like that?" Wilma sighed. "Just as well Cherish isn't here, or she'd make me keep you, but I'm not. Did you hear me? I'm not keeping you."

Red lowered himself to the floor but kept his eyes on Wilma.

"Still, I must keep pretending to like you." Wilma leaned down and whispered, "Because of Obadiah."

The dog lunged up and licked her up the side of her face.

"Oh." Wilma jumped up and raced over to the sink to wash her face. "This is why it'll never work between us," Wilma said as she dried her face with a cloth.

Wilma quickly backed away from the dog when she heard someone coming down the stairs. She didn't want anyone to know she'd been talking to a dog.

Debbie walked into the kitchen, followed by Jared. Jared saw the dog and ran to it.

"Careful, Jared. We still don't know if it bites," Wilma cautioned.

Debbie's eyebrows drew together. "Is someone else here?"

"No, just me."

"I thought I heard you talking to someone."

Wilma shook her head. "You might've heard Matthew talking to himself. He's most likely still out there on the porch."

Debbie giggled. "Possibly. Nothing with him would surprise me."

Wilma grinned, glad Matthew had come in handy for something. "Hot tea before I start the breakfast, Debbie?"

"Yes, please."

SIMON and his father were passing the time by painting the outside of the house. Favor had changed her mind about the color half a dozen times, but she'd settled on a particular shade of pale green. She felt it went well with the surroundings and would blend seamlessly.

Simon couldn't wait for her to see it when she felt better. He painted alongside Melvin, who was perched precariously atop a ladder several feet away.

Simon would never share this with Favor, but he felt that his parents' arrival had been a blessing.

He had never lived independently before, and he was also concerned about being able to support his family. It burdened him in ways that only a man could understand.

With his folks around, he knew they'd help out. Each day he prayed for harmony between Favor and his parents, hoping for a peaceful relationship. But their presence also brought new anxieties. Favor was expecting a baby, and he wasn't sure if Harriet's hovering and overbearing ways would cause Favor too much stress.

Simon heard the clip-clopping of a horse's hooves and turned to see Zeke and Emma approaching. He walked over and welcomed them warmly.

"I see you're working. We can come back another time," Zeke said.

"No, that's fine. We're ready for a break."

"That's good because I came to speak with you and your father."

"Okay, let's go inside."

The four of them made their way inside. Simon and his father sat with Zeke while Emma went to the kitchen to find Favor, but she was met by Harriet. Emma was taken aback by what Harriet was doing.

Harriet was in the middle of painting a single row of flowers along the kitchen walls. The flowers were in varying colors— shades of purple to bright greens that contrasted with the pale background. "Hello, Harriet."

Harriet straightened up. "Hello, Emma. Nice to see you again."

"This is different. Did Favor come up with this idea?"

"No, it's a surprise for her, for when she's better. She's sick in bed."

"I'm sorry to hear that. I would've brought some soup over if I'd known."

"No. I can make soup. She hasn't mentioned anything about soup. Why? Did someone say something about her wanting soup?"

"No. It's just when I'm sick that I like soup."

"I see. Are you here by yourself?"

"No. Zeke's here too. He came to talk to Simon and his father." Emma frowned, unsure if Favor would agree with having painted flowers on her freshly painted kitchen wall. "Do you know what's wrong with Favor?"

"Nothing contagious, I hope, or we'll all be sick. Then you can bring the soup over." Harriet chuckled as she placed her paintbrush down and put the lids back on the paints. "I'll finish this later. So, Emma. I know we've been introduced at the Sunday meeting, but I want to ask you something."

Emma sat down at the table. "Sure."

"Just how close are you with Favor?"

"Zeke and I met them when they were visiting before they moved here. Now we've probably seen them every day."

"Has she mentioned anything about this sickness to you?"

Emma shook her head. "No. I haven't seen her for a couple of days. She was fine then."

Harriet looked back at the wall. "I hope she likes this. That gray was so dull and boring. Favor is not dull and boring. I think this will make it look like it's Spring all year-'round." Harriet stood back from the walls to admire her handiwork.

In the living room, Simon asked, "What brings you by today, Zeke?"

"I want to continue the talk from the other day. I've got a business idea you might be interested in."

Simon perked up in his seat, and Melvin leaned forward eagerly.

"A business proposal? That's great!" Simon exclaimed.

Melvin joined in. "Let's hear it then!"

Zeke grinned and discussed the three of them going into business together.

"Like join in a kind of a co-op?" Melvin asked.

"I guess you could say that. We'll only do this if it's the right thing for all of us and if the bishop allows you to have that last parcel of land, Melvin."

"There could be a problem. I heard the land was only for couples or young families. That's what we were told," Simon said.

"I'm going to ask if we might buy it. Minds can always be changed," Melvin said.

Zeke sat back in his seat. "We'll have to wait and see."

"It sounds like a good idea. If we can't buy it, I'll just help Simon. I've got a lot of good years left in me yet."

Zeke nodded with confidence. "With God's help, we can make it a success."

Melvin raised his eyebrows. "If the bishop permits us to purchase the land, we'll build our house closer to the road, minimizing our impact on farming space. That way, you two won't have to spend money on the land."

Simon felt a knot in his stomach, uncertain about Favor's reaction to his parents being so nearby. It had been her one condition. "We'll have to discuss it with the women first, but I'm excited about the idea."

"Count me in, too," Melvin added. "We'll have another family meeting to discuss it. Once we have the ladies' approval and if the bishop allows us to proceed, it must make sense financially. We'll have to crunch some numbers."

Zeke stood up. "I can show you my financial projections for my current work and run future projections for the three of us combined."

The other men rose to their feet as well. "Yes, that's a good idea," Melvin said, nodding.

"I'll head out now. I just wanted to share my idea," Zeke said. The men shook hands just as Emma and Harriet entered the room.

"Is everything okay here?" Emma inquired.

"Yeah, we're just discussing farming," Simon explained.

"That sounds interesting," Harriet chimed in with a smile. "I'd love to see adorable alpacas grazing in the fields."

"Me too," Emma nodded, echoing the sentiment. "I mean, at your place, because I already have them there... at my place."

Simon noticed that Emma appeared nervous. It seemed like everyone was tense around his mother.

Once Zeke and Emma departed, Simon headed to the bedroom to check on Favor's well-being. However, something in the kitchen caught his attention, causing him to halt in his tracks.

Colorful flowers were painted along the kitchen walls. His gaze then fell upon small paint cans. Removing the design would require numerous coats of paint. A lump formed in his throat at the thought of how upset Favor would be.

His mother had crossed a line.

Maintaining peace between his mother and Favor would become even more challenging.

LATER IN THE DAY, Simon sat on a chair, his fingers nervously tapping against the wooden armrest. The room was filled with anticipation for the important family meeting. Favor was out of bed for the occasion, wrapped in a blanket, and still looking quite pale.

The aroma of freshly brewed coffee wafted through the air, momentarily soothing their restless minds.

"Alright, everyone," Simon began, clearing his throat. "Pa and I have been thinking about something for a while now, and we'd like to discuss it."

Harriet raised an eyebrow, her hazel eyes filled with curiosity. "Well, don't hold back, Simon. What's on your mind?"

Melvin leaned forward, his eyes gleaming with excitement. "It's about our neighbors, Zachary and Emma."

"We call him Zeke or Zac," Simon said.

"That's right. Zeke." Melvin nodded.

Simon continued, "They've started an alpaca farm, and I've been doing some research. It seems like a profitable business, and I think we should consider joining them."

Harriet tilted her head, her expression thoughtful. "There's been an awful lot of talk about alpacas since we arrived. But what exactly does it entail?"

Simon reached for the pile of papers he had gathered, unfolding them to reveal statistics that Zeke had given them. "Alpacas are known for their soft wool, which is highly sought after in the textile industry. Our neighbors have already started breeding and selling them, and there's a growing market for their products."

Harriet's eyes sparkled with curiosity as she skimmed through the paperwork. "And how do they fit into our lives, Simon? It sounds intriguing, but we need to consider the time and resources required."

Simon nodded. "I've thought about that, too. Zeke and Emma have offered their expertise and even offered to share their land for the initial stages. It wouldn't be an easy endeavor, but with careful planning and dedication, it could become a sustainable business for all of us."

Melvin interjected with an enthusiastic smile, "Think about it, Harriet, the alpaca business could bring us all closer. We'd be working with Simon again.

We could work together, supporting each other, and build something meaningful for the future."

"Pa and I want to tell Zeke we're in it with him, but we just need you both to agree." He looked at his mother and then Favor.

Harriet leaned back in her chair, her gaze distant as she considered the proposition. "We've been looking for a way to spend more time together as a family. And if the neighbors are willing to help, perhaps we can give it a try."

Simon grinned and then looked at his wife. "Favor?"

"I trust your judgment. If you and Pa believe in this, then I agree. Besides, we don't have anything else right at this moment."

"Thank you. Pa and I will do everything we can to make this work."

"I know you will. You're both such hard workers," Harriet said.

Melvin's face beamed with excitement. "Then it's settled! We'll speak to the neighbors and start planning. This could be the beginning of something remarkable."

"Can I go back to bed now?" Favor whined. "I'm not feeling the best."

Harriet jumped to her feet. "Of course. I'll walk you there. Can I get you anything?" Harriet asked as she looped her arm through Favor's arm.

Harriet guided Favor out of the room, their footsteps fading as they made their way down the hallway.

Simon, Melvin, and the lingering aroma of coffee remained behind.

Melvin glanced at Simon, gratitude evident in his eyes. "I'm glad you're on board, son. This means a lot to me."

"Me too. We can work together again. And with Ma and Favor by our side, it feels like we're finally coming together as a family again."

Melvin nodded, his voice filled with determination. "This alpaca venture could be the fresh start we've been yearning for. We'll make it a success, not just for ourselves but for our family's future."

Simon felt a little guilty for keeping the secret from his folks about the baby. They had to keep the news to themselves for just a few more weeks.

As they sipped their coffee, a renewed sense of purpose filled the room.

Harriet returned to the room, her expression warm. "Favor is settled in bed, resting. She'll recover in no time."

Simon smiled at his mother. "Thank you, Ma. You always take care of us."

Harriet's eyes twinkled with affection. "That's what mothers do. This alpaca business sounds exciting."

Simon nodded. "I can't wait to get started."

CHAPTER 24

*O*n Friday morning, Bliss dedicated a few hours to work at Debbie's tea stall so that Debbie and Fritz could have some alone time before Jared finished school.

Just before midday, Fritz arrived to pick up Debbie, and they drove to the park together. Once they arrived, they found a secluded spot near the pond and spread out a picnic blanket. Fritz unpacked a basket filled with an assortment of food, offering Debbie a sandwich before laying out an array of cheeses, bread, condiments, and cherry drops.

Debbie couldn't help but giggle at all the food Fritz had brought. "That's enough to feed the entire community!"

"Only the best for you," he replied, handing her the cherry drops.

"Thank you. How did you know they were my favorite?" Debbie asked, pleasantly surprised.

"I listen to you," Fritz answered, his eyes filled with affection.

"Did you make all of this?"

"My mother gave me a helping hand," Fritz confessed.

"That was nice of her."

"She saw me packing and decided to lend a hand. She didn't think I was doing a good job." He chuckled.

"Please tell her thank you from me."

"I will. She loves you very much," Fritz whispered softly.

"I love her too." Debbie's smile faded quickly as thoughts of the impending wedding began to weigh on her. The constant inquiries from others about the wedding plans had started to unsettle her. Nothing had been set in stone yet, and this uncertainty caused unease to well up inside her.

Fritz saw her face. "What's wrong?"

"It's nothing much. I don't want to worry you," she replied.

"You can tell me. I'm here to help. So, what is it?" Fritz encouraged her.

"Everyone keeps asking about our wedding date. We still haven't chosen one," she confessed, trying to keep uncertainty from seeping through her words.

Fritz responded cautiously, "You're right... we

haven't decided on a date yet... and it's not too far off anymore."

Debbie gave a slight nod. They had initially decided to do it by the end of the year. She didn't want him to feel pressured. "If you think it's too soon, we can always postpone it until next year."

"No, I said it would be this year. What do you say about December 3rd?"

Debbie was relieved and knew everything would be okay. "December 3rd works for me," she responded.

"Good. I'll contact the bishop tomorrow, and I'm sure he'll give his consent for that day." Fritz reclined on his elbows and stared out at the lake. "I've been wondering where we'd end up living once we're married. I scrolled through some homes in the newspaper. I'm not positive that we will have one ready in time."

"That's all right. We can stay with Wilma at the orchard as long as need be. She's already offered that."

"No, that won't be necessary. It's proven to be more challenging than I imagined tying up loose ends and moving here. Everything will work out, though, and I'll find us something to move into."

"That's fine with me. As long as we're together, nothing else matters. Jared is so excited that you're here." Debbie took a bite of her sandwich.

Fritz smiled widely. "It's been too long since I last saw you both."

Debbie swallowed hard and grinned at him. "I can't wait until you're here to stay."

He held her hand. "Me either, and hopefully soon, we will have a baby, a brother or sister, for Jared to play with."

Debbie was overjoyed by what she heard. "Jared would love that."

Fritz gave her hand a gentle squeeze, sending warmth through her body. She couldn't believe how everything had worked out for the best. Fritz was about to become her husband, Jared was thriving in school, and her tea business became more popular daily.

Everything was just as it should be.

lorence sat on the couch, nursing her baby boy. Iris was outside playing in the garden with Spot, their dog.

Carter brought Florence a glass of water and sat down with her. "How are you feeling?"

"Good. It's helped to have the night nurse. I wouldn't be feeling better if I hadn't had such a good sleep. I'm so glad you thought about that."

"Sleep is everything when you have a baby," Carter said.

Florence looked down at her new son and smiled. "He's so quiet. It's as if nothing bothers him."

"Takes after me, I'd say." Carter chuckled.

"Maybe. Did you see how Wilma teared up when she held him?"

"No."

"I'd say she was thinking about you and how she gave you up."

Carter shook his head. "I don't know about that. I think she's put all that right out of her head. Still, it's nice that she's allowing me to help her with those houses Levi left her."

"I know. It's a start in the right direction. The older I get, the more I realize how hard everything was for Wilma." Florence held her baby a little bit closer. "I couldn't imagine being forced to give up my baby due to other people's expectations. Things were so different back then." She stroked her baby's soft cheek.

"Would it be any different today in your community?" Carter asked.

Florence thought about that for a while. "I'm not sure. Maybe not. The community probably hasn't changed too much."

"I'm glad you left."

Florence looked up at him and smiled. "I had to. You would never have joined."

"You got that right. So much of it doesn't make sense."

Florence was in no mood to discuss Carter's atheist beliefs. She always prayed that one day he'd know that God was real. "How is Iris coming along with the name? Has she come up with anything yet?"

Carter grimaced. "Nothing I'd like to tell you."

"Oh no. Is it bad?"

"I'm not so sure if it was a good idea to let her choose the baby's name."

"Well, we talked about it, and we both decided it would make her feel included. I was the youngest child, and then my father married Wilma, and I wasn't the baby anymore. It did affect me."

He put his hand lovingly on her shoulder. "I know. Well, I don't know. Growing up as an only child, I got loads of attention, but I can imagine how it was for you."

The baby began to fuss as they sat there, and Florence shifted to cradle him more comfortably. "Shh, it's alright," she murmured, rocking him gently.

Carter watched her with a soft smile, feeling his heart swell with love for both of them.

Suddenly, the sound of Iris shouting grabbed their attention. "Help! Dad! Spot caught a rabbit!"

Carter stood up, alarmed, and rushed out the door. "Did he hurt it?"

"I don't know." Iris burst into tears.

Carter grabbed Spot's collar. "I think he's just holding it in his mouth!"

"Where's Mommy?"

Florence stood up with the baby and called out, "I'm coming."

When Florence was outside, she saw Iris kneeling in the grass, Spot beside her, his tail wagging happily. In his mouth was a small rabbit, keeping very still.

"Can I keep the bunny?"

Florence shook her head. "No. We have to let it go back into the wild."

Iris frowned, looking down at the rabbit. "But I want to keep it! It's so cute!" Then the tears started again. "Has Spot hurt it?"

Carter looked down at the rabbit and tried to pry open Spot's mouth. He hoped that the rabbit was unharmed. He didn't want Iris to see anything awful. "I know it's cute, but it's not fair to the rabbit to keep it cooped up in a cage. It deserves to be free, to run around and play with its friends."

Florence said, "Once Dad gets it away from Spot, we can always come outside and try to find it again."

Iris brightened up. "Can we do that?"

"Of course, sweetie. But we have to let it go now."

With a heavy heart, Iris nodded. They watched as Carter commanded Spot to sit, and Spot obediently released his hold on the rabbit. Like a lightning bolt, the freed animal scampered away into the safety of the bushes.

Just as Spot made to bolt after it, Carter grabbed his collar, halting him.

Florence had never been fond of rabbits, but for Iris's sake, she felt a wave of relief wash over her, knowing it was unharmed.

"Maybe we shouldn't have let it go," Florence mused. "Next time, we'll catch it and give it to Bliss. She appreciates rabbits."

"Yes. She certainly does love her rabbits," Carter replied.

"As cute as they may seem, rabbits can wreak havoc in an orchard. I'll have Fairfax attend to that. We certainly don't need a rabbit plague."

Carter agreed with a nod. He then shifted his gaze down to Iris and hoisted her into his arms. "Have you thought of any names for the baby?"

"I've thought of the perfect name!" she exclaimed.

Carter raised an eyebrow. "Oh, really? Let's hear it."

Iris took a deep breath and said, "I'm calling him Chess."

Florence's eyes widened in surprise. "Chess? Like the board game?"

Iris nodded eagerly. "Exactly! Daddy loves that game. It's all about strategy and bravery. Chess will be strong and courageous. He'll light up our lives like a fire and destroy all our enemies."

Florence frowned, not appreciating the talk of violence. "There aren't any enemies, dear. If there were, we'd let God handle them. But I think I like the name Chess."

Carter exchanged a glance with Florence, uncertainty evident in his eyes. "It's an unconventional name, to say the least."

Florence pondered a moment. "If Iris likes it, maybe we should consider it."

Iris jumped up and down. "Yes! Chess it is! You said I could name him, and that's the name I choose."

Carter's smile was gentle, his decision already made. "Alright then, Chess it is."

Florence chuckled as she gazed down at her sleeping baby. "Well, Chess, you've got quite the name to live up to. You'll need to be big and strong," she murmured.

Enthusiastically, Iris added, "That's right, and he'll slay enemies just like in the game of chess."

Florence's brows knitted in a frown. "There'll be no slaying going on. Where do you hear such things?"

"From the chess games and the stories Dad reads me," Iris responded.

Florence turned to look at Carter, who just shrugged in response. "I haven't noticed anything too concerning."

"I dislike the violence," Florence stated.

"Oh, Mom, they're just stories. They're not real," Iris argued.

"Still..." Florence's voice trailed off, leaving her thoughts unfinished.

Carter grinned. "We won't read any more of those stories, okay, Iris?"

"Okay," Iris conceded.

The rest of the day unfolded without incident. Florence and Carter attended to Chess while Iris played with Spot in the garden.

It was after an early dinner that Iris voiced her boredom. "There's nothing to do. I'm bored," she whined, flopping onto the couch next to Florence.

Florence smiled sympathetically. "I know, sweetie. But we can't stay entertained all the time. Besides, sometimes it's nice to do nothing. When I was your age, I had so many chores I never had time to do anything else. There was no time to be bored."

"Why did you have so many chores?"

"There was so much to do. We didn't have the things that we do. We didn't have a dishwasher, for instance. We had to wash everything by hand, and the same for our clothes."

"Why?"

Carter, who had been flipping through a book, looked up. "I could read you a story if you'd like."

Iris brightened. "Yes, please!"

Florence frowned. "What kind of story?"

Carter stood up and went over to the shelf, scanning the titles. His eyes fell on a collection of fairy tales, and he pulled it down. "How about a fairy tale?" He glanced over at Florence and added, "A non-violent one."

Iris nodded eagerly, settling in beside Florence. Carter cleared his throat and began to read. His voice was deep and soothing, and soon all three of them were lost in the magical world of the story. They journeyed through enchanted forests and outwitted cunning villains as the tale unfolded. Iris sat with her eyes wide open, completely absorbed in the story.

As the story drew to a close, Carter's voice became

softer. "And they all lived happily ever after," he finished.

Florence was pleased the tale had been gentle. "Thank you for that."

Carter grinned back at her. "Anytime. Now it's bedtime, Iris."

Iris groaned. "Do I have to?"

Florence chuckled. "Yes, sweetie. We all need our sleep."

As they got up to head to bed, Florence couldn't help but feel grateful for the simple joys of family life. She tucked Chess into his crib and watched as he snuggled into his blanket, his tiny fist closing around it.

Her heart filled with so much love she thought she'd simply burst.

She leaned down and pressed a kiss to his forehead. "Goodnight, Chess."

Iris climbed into her own bed, still mulling over the fairy tale in her head. "I wish I could have an adventure like that," she sighed.

Carter chuckled. "Who says you can't? With a little imagination, anything is possible."

Iris grinned, already picturing herself as a brave princess on a daring quest.

The night nurse arrived and went quietly to the baby's room.

Sometime later, Florence climbed into bed beside Carter, feeling his arm settle around her.

"What do you think Wilma will say when we tell her the baby's name?"

Florence giggled. "She'll smile and say it's nice. Then later on, she'll talk to Ada about how unsuitable it is."

"Everyone will get used to it."

"I know. I like it more already."

"Me too."

Florence closed her eyes, feeling the warmth of his body against hers. It was moments like this that made her feel safe and loved. She drifted off to sleep, feeling content and at peace.

CHAPTER 26

The next morning, Florence woke up to the sound of chirping birds outside her window. As she yawned and stretched, she realized that something felt off. She turned to Carter, who was still sleeping beside her, and shook his shoulder gently. "Carter, wake up."

Carter groaned and blinked his eyes open. "What is it?"

"I don't know. Something just doesn't feel right."

Carter sat up, rubbing his eyes. "What do you mean?"

Florence shook her head. "I don't know. Maybe I'm just being paranoid."

Carter frowned. "Do you want me to check on the children?"

Florence nodded, suddenly feeling anxious. "Yes."

Carter got out of bed and quickly went to the baby's room.

A moment later, he returned to the bedroom, his face white as a sheet. "Florence, Wilma is in the kitchen. She said the night nurse let her in."

As Florence went to the kitchen, she caught a whiff of something delicious coming from the oven. Her mouth watered as she realized it was Wilma's famous blueberry muffins.

She found Wilma busily cooking breakfast. "Good morning, Wilma. Those muffins smell amazing!"

Wilma smiled, her eyes crinkling at the corners. "Good morning, Florence. I know how much you love them. I thought I'd surprise you."

Florence hugged her, grateful for Wilma's kindness. "Thank you so much. You're the best."

Wilma chuckled. "I know how tiring it can be having young babies. I just wanted to do a little something for you."

"I'm surprised to see you."

Florence couldn't help but feel grateful for Wilma as they sat down to breakfast. She was doing her best to patch up old wounds.

Iris was delighted to wake up and see Wilma at the house and even more delighted to taste Wilma's baking.

Wilma got a chance to hold the baby when the night nurse left.

Wilma laughed when she put her finger in the

baby's hand, and he wrapped his fingers tightly around it. "He's so sweet. You just forget how small they are at this age. Have you named him yet? Everyone's been asking."

"We have," Carter said.

Wilma looked up, bracing herself for a name chosen by a child. "Well, what is it?"

"We've named him Chess."

Wilma's face stayed expressionless. "Chess?"

"It's Dad's favorite game," Iris said.

"It is the game that made me my first mill... that gave me a good head start, financially."

Wilma stared at Carter. "You've named your baby after a game?"

Carter smiled. "I know. It's a bit unusual, but you'll get used to it. Wait a minute." Carter pulled out his phone and tapped a couple of things into it. "I just googled it. It is a boy's name. So, we're not the first ones to use it."

Wilma breathed out heavily, and Florence noticed that she was troubled. "Chess Braithwaite," Wilma said slowly. "Hmm."

Carter and Florence glanced over at each other and smiled.

That was all that was said about the name.

Iris then told Wilma all about the rabbit that had visited them.

When breakfast was over, Wilma announced she had to get home.

"I'll drive you back, Wilma," Carter offered.

"No. It's not far. I prefer to walk on a nice morning like this. I'll go back through the orchard rather than walk down the road."

They all stood at the door to wave her off.

"Be careful of rabbits!" Iris called out.

Wilma turned back and waved and then kept walking as she muttered to herself, "Rabbits, stray dogs, what's next?"

Wilma arrived home to see Ada sitting on the porch with Red at her feet. When Ada saw her approaching the house, she stood up and leaned on the porch railing. Red got up, saw Wilma, and bounded toward her. "Where have you been?" Ada asked.

"I was over at Florence's house. I made them breakfast." Wilma stepped up on the porch. "I'm sorry. I didn't know you'd be here so early."

"Humph. Don't you start saying you're sorry for everything. I'll have to start calling you Susan."

Wilma smiled as she pushed open the front door. "Come in, and I'll make us a pot of tea."

As they sat down at the kitchen table, sipping tea, Wilma announced, "They've come up with a name for the baby."

Ada's eyes popped wide open. "What is it?"

"It's a name Iris picked out."

"Oh no!" Ada put her teacup down in the saucer and held her head. "Just how bad is it, Wilma?"

Wilma looked down. "I'll let you decide."

"Don't keep me waiting. What is it?"

"Chess."

"Chess?" Ada made a face.

"That's right. The baby's name is Chess Braithwaite."

"Oh, Wilma. That's dreadful, simply horrid. Did you tell them you disapprove?"

"No. I hardly think they'd care what I thought. I didn't want to upset Iris. She was there in the room when they told me."

"What about a middle name? If the child had a sensible middle name, he could lose the name Chess when he gets older."

"They never mentioned a middle name," Wilma said.

"Did you ask?"

"No. I think they would've said if they'd had one. Carter likes the name because he had that chess game that he developed. It made him millions."

Ada's mouth turned down at the corners. "I don't like it. People are naming their children after the passions that drive them. What happened to naming a child after their ancestors?"

"They did do that with Iris."

"That's true, after your sister, but they could've called the baby Josiah after Florence's father. What about that, eh?"

Wilma nodded in agreement, thinking about her

first husband. "I think that would've been a great name."

Ada stood up and walked over to the window, and gazed out. "It's a shame. Josiah Braithwaite sounds like a pleasant name."

Wilma got up and joined her at the window. "Maybe we can convince them to change it. After all, the baby doesn't know his name yet."

Ada turned around, a hopeful look on her face. "Do you think we could?"

"We won't know until we try." Wilma smiled at her friend. "Let's pay them a visit and see if we can persuade them to choose a more fitting name."

Ada nodded in agreement, her eyes lighting up with determination. "Yes, let's do it. We can't let that poor child go through life with a name like Chess."

They quickly finished their tea. Wilma closed Red in the mudroom so he wouldn't follow, and then they walked briskly down the road to Florence and Carter's house.

CHAPTER 27

When they arrived at the house, they found Florence and Carter sitting on the front porch, admiring their newborn son while Iris dug in the garden with a plastic spade.

"Hi there, ladies," Carter greeted them with a smile.

Iris looked up, saw them, and ran to hug them both.

"Oh yes. We also came to talk to you about the baby's name," Ada said firmly, not wasting any time.

Florence asked, "You don't like the name we chose?"

"It's not a name that will serve him well in life," Wilma said. "People might think he's named after a board game, or worse."

Carter looked taken aback. "I never thought of that. But I don't want to change his name. It's unique, and it means something to us."

"I chose it," Iris said. "Don't you like it?"

165

Wilma looked down at her granddaughter and didn't want to hurt her feelings. "I do."

"But what about a middle name?" Ada suggested, moving closer to admire the baby. "Something more traditional, like Josiah, after your father, Florence."

Florence looked thoughtful. "I do like the sound of Josiah for the middle name. Here, Ada, would you like to hold the baby?"

Ada's face lit up as she took the newborn into her arms. "He's delightful."

Carter rubbed his chin. "I suppose we could consider it. Chess Josiah Braithwaite has a nice flow."

Wilma and Ada looked at each other, smiling. "It's settled, then," Wilma said. "Chess Josiah Braithwaite it is."

"Perfect." Florence nodded and looked over at Carter, who added his agreement. "Can you stay for a while?" Florence asked them.

"We should be getting back. Ada has some problems with Matthew to sort out."

"What's happening with Matthew?" Carter asked.

Wilma didn't want Florence to see him in a bad light since she was technically his boss. She was the one with the biggest say in the orchard. "Nothing, not much."

"Nothing to do with work," Ada added. "Come along, Wilma. We should go."

"Yes."

Ada carefully passed the baby to Florence.

As they stepped back, Carter offered to drive them both home. They said they'd enjoy the walk.

Once Ada and Wilma were out of sight, Florence and Carter looked over at each other and burst out laughing.

"I was sure you were going to tell them we'd already chosen Josiah for his middle name," Florence said.

"No way. I didn't want to spoil the fun."

"Aw, how come I didn't get to choose his middle name too?" Iris asked.

"It's just a middle name," Florence told her. "It's not as important as the first name."

"Yes. Nowhere near as important," Carter said.

As Ada and Wilma walked back down the road, Ada couldn't help but feel good about giving the child a better option. "I'm glad we were able to convince them," Ada said, grinning from ear to ear.

"It just goes to show that sometimes, it's good to speak up and challenge what bothers you," Wilma replied.

Ada nodded in agreement. "Exactly. We can't just sit by and let things happen. We must act and say what we think is right."

Wilma smiled at her friend's determination. "Maybe we should say something to Matthew now that we feel empowered like this."

"We'll have to wait until tonight. Now, I do have something else to tell you about."

"What?"

"I told you I sent a few letters to some of my friends asking them about Obadiah, didn't I?"

"You didn't have to do that." Wilma was worried that it would get back to Obadiah that Ada was asking questions behind his back.

"I heard back from one of my friends and she only had good things to say. I know you like him, and I can see that he feels the same. I'm just trying to protect you from getting your heart broken."

When they reached the bottom of the driveway, Wilma looked over at the shop they used to open in the warmer months. "Someone should open that shop again."

"We'll do it, Wilma."

Wilma bit her lip. "Do you think we should?"

"Why not? Wasn't that what we decided last year?"

"Possibly. My memory is a bit fuzzy these days. It'll be a big commitment. It'll keep us from doing our charity work."

"Well, somehow, we can work the two in together. We can get others to help."

Wilma smiled. "You're right. Let's do it! We can do anything when we set our minds to it."

As they continued walking, Ada was excited about the future. They were making a difference in their community, and now they had a new project to work on.

Suddenly, Ada was troubled when she heard a

rustling in the bushes. She stopped in her tracks, and Wilma noticed her sudden change in demeanor.

"What's wrong?" Wilma asked.

"I heard something in the bushes."

Wilma looked over and saw Red scratching around. "It's only Red." Wilma called to him, and he came over. "I thought we closed you in the mudroom."

"You probably didn't close the door properly. You haven't found a home for him yet, Wilma?"

"No, but I will."

CHAPTER 28

*D*ebbie was working at her tea stall, delighted with having a definite date for her wedding. She would soon be Mrs. White, and Jared would have a proper family structure.

During a lull between customers, she busied herself rearranging the display of tea boxes.

Feeling a presence behind her, she turned, expecting to find a customer waiting.

To her surprise, it was her soon-to-be brother-in-law, Peter.

"Did you and Fritz enjoy your time together?" he asked.

"We did," she replied, wondering why he was there.

"I trust you liked the cherry drops—I remembered they were your favorites, so I included them in the basket."

A chill crept down Debbie's spine at his words. "The cherry drops were your idea?"

"Yes."

Peter suddenly seemed like a stranger. An awkward silence hung between them, and Debbie found it hard to meet his gaze.

"Debbie," he started, breaking the silence, "I'll be direct. Why do you believe Fritz is the right man for you?"

Debbie's brow furrowed in confusion. "What do you mean?"

Peter took a deep breath. "How can you be so certain that Fritz is the one for you?"

With a guarded expression, Debbie countered, "I'm not sure I want to discuss this with you, Peter."

Peter straightened, pulling back his shoulders. "You rejected me for years and then fell for my older brother within a matter of weeks. You owe me an explanation, Debbie."

Debbie instinctively stepped back, her hand beginning to tremble. She had never seen Peter behave in such a manner. Noticing her apprehension, he softened his stance.

"I apologize for raising my voice. I just think you should be aware that he might not follow through."

"With what?" she asked, her voice barely a whisper.

"With this whole marriage scenario... I don't think he's cut out for it," Peter blurted out.

Debbie felt a pang of disappointment hearing Peter speak so badly about his own brother. "Please leave, Peter. This conversation is not one we should be having."

"He doesn't truly know you, and you don't know him! He's never been one to settle down. He's a lifelong bachelor," Peter insisted. "Some of us are bachelors beyond our control, but he's always been one by choice."

Debbie couldn't believe the words tumbling out of Peter's mouth. All she could do was stare at him.

"I won't leave until you explain. Why him and not me?" he demanded.

It seemed the words escaped her lips before she could stop them. "Just as well I didn't choose you."

"Why?" he asked, a hint of desperation creeping into his voice.

Debbie crossed her arms defensively. "Have you forgotten about Maisy?"

Taken aback, Peter stepped away. "No, I'm happy with her."

"Then why are you here? What do you want from me?" Debbie asked.

"You made me feel unloved and unlovable. It was Maisy who showed me that I am worthy of love," Peter admitted.

Debbie was at her wits' end. He wouldn't leave, and she was at a loss for what to do. "I'm in love with Fritz. I don't know what else you want me to say. How can a person explain why they love someone and not someone else? There's nothing wrong with you."

Peter was silent momentarily, as if time had frozen around him. Finally, he spoke. "I'm going back home. You two won't hear from me again."

As Peter walked away, Debbie sank into the chair behind her counter. How would she explain all this to Fritz?

She just hoped she wouldn't be blamed for coming between brothers. A tear slipped down Debbie's cheek. How she wished Fritz was there to comfort her.

CHAPTER 29

*A*fter the Sunday meeting, Wilma sat with her friends, and Fritz and Debbie were also there.

"Peter's not here today?" Wilma asked. "I didn't see him in the meeting."

Fritz shrugged his shoulders. "He took off back home without saying a word. I gather it was something to do with Maisy."

Debbie bit her lip as she avoided making eye contact with anyone. How would she tell him that Peter had attempted to get some kind of resolution before he left in a rage?

She knew she had to tell Fritz the truth eventually.

Wilma cleared her throat. "Fritz, I don't know if you two have already figured out where you will live after the wedding, but you're both welcome to stay at the orchard for as long as necessary."

"Thank you, Wilma. That's most kind of you. I've

been keeping busy looking around for houses to buy. None have caught my attention yet, and it might take a while before I get something that suits our needs."

That comment caught Wilma off guard. What if he didn't like the house she planned to give them?

She had never considered that his standards might be higher than the humble cottage. "You're moving your entire life for Debbie, so it's only fair we do what we can to help."

Debbie smiled warmly at Wilma.

Leaving the meeting, Matthew was overcome with bitterness. He felt a deep sense of isolation, realizing that he had no one to sit with. All his friends were also friends with Krystal, and now he felt displaced. Sitting with Fairfax was not an option either, as Sigrid was always near Fairfax and Hope.

No matter where he looked, he saw Krystal and Jed engaged in lively conversations and laughter. Sigrid and Andrew seemed to be enjoying each other's company as well. Every scene served as a painful reminder of his failure, although he couldn't pinpoint exactly how he had reached this point.

Jealousy clawed at Matthew from two directions like nothing he'd ever felt before. He decided to go back to the orchard and wait for Krystal. She'd show up eventually, and hopefully, she'd be alone.

As he climbed into his buggy, he spotted Sigrid returning to the house while Andrew climbed into his buggy.

What had happened? They were usually together every moment.

Was there a quarrel between the two of them? Taking advantage of the opportunity, Matthew quickly drove his buggy forward and pulled up alongside Andrew's. "Hey, how are you doing, Andrew?"

Andrew looked over at him. "I'm doing well. How about yourself?"

"I'm alright. You're not taking Sigrid home today?"

"Yes, she'll be here in a minute."

"I don't see her."

"She forgot something and went back to get it."

Matthew curled his lip in irritation. "That's nice. You two look good together."

"That's kind of you to say so. I hope this isn't uncomfortable for you in any way," Andrew said.

"What's that?" Matthew asked.

"Seeing me with Sigrid after she ended things with you. You're probably upset."

"Upset? No way. I consider myself a family man. It was the hardest decision I've ever had to make, but when I discovered that Sigrid couldn't have children, I knew there was no other option but to end things with her. So you see, it was me who ended things."

Andrew lifted his brows in disbelief. "What was that about children?"

"Oh. She hasn't told you yet?"

"I'm not sure I heard you right. Could you repeat what you just said?"

"I said Sigrid can't have children."

Andrew's face fell.

Matthew spotted Sigrid coming toward the buggy, so he whipped his horse with the reins. "Nice seeing you, Andrew. Have a good day!" Matthew called over his shoulder as the horse took off at a trot.

CHAPTER 30

*E*ver since Jed's confrontation with Matthew, he had been hesitant to approach the bishop for permission to drive a bus. Yet, he needed the bishop's approval for the next phase. The meetings were never the right place to ask the bishop anything—he was always surrounded by people.

Late that Sunday afternoon, Jed borrowed Samuel's buggy and went to the bishop's house.

As soon as he arrived, the bishop opened the door. "Jed, you were on my mind," he greeted him, his tone stern.

Jed wondered why. "Why were you thinking of me?"

"We'll get to that. Please, come in and have a seat."

Jed followed the bishop into the kitchen, where they seated themselves at opposite ends of the table. The bishop's wife, Hannah, served them cups of hot tea before retreating, leaving the men to their conversation.

"I know you're new to our town," the bishop started, "and I understand you intend to marry Krystal, correct?"

"Yes, that's right," Jed confirmed. "We get along very well, and we believe it's God's will for us to take the next step."

"She's come a long way. I've watched her transform into a strong woman of faith," the bishop noted.

Jed nodded in agreement, unsure where the bishop was steering the conversation.

"I wouldn't want her to fall back into her past ways," the bishop said, staring at Jed under his bushy eyebrows.

"I agree," replied Jed. "Nobody would want that."

"Did you come here to discuss Krystal?"

"No, not exactly. It's about something else." Jed paused for a moment. "Well, yes, about asking permission to marry Krystal and another matter. But I'll return another time to discuss Krystal."

"Proceed," the bishop prompted.

"Well, we've been brainstorming. I need work, so Krystal and I thought up an idea. We'd like to offer tours of the Baker Apple Orchard, the surrounding district, and possibly a few other local businesses too, like the beekeepers. I know the beekeepers aren't members of our community, but they are local."

"And?" the bishop inquired.

Jed hesitated, his nervousness suddenly making his throat feel dry. "Well, we... I mean I... was thinking that if we had a way to transport more people than a horse-drawn cart could..."

"What are you suggesting?"

"Well, if we had a bus, it could accommodate more passengers than a wagon," Jed said.

"A bus?" The bishop's eyebrows shot up. "I suppose you want to drive this bus?"

"Yes, that was my thought."

The bishop shook his head decisively. "It's out of the question. We cannot go against our community's traditions. It wouldn't be fair to give the impression that we operate motor vehicles like the rest of the world."

Jed was taken aback by the bishop's stern refusal without giving it some careful thought. Usually, he had a knack for persuasion, but his skills seemed ineffective now. "I only mentioned it because I've heard of some communities where the bishop permits farmers to drive tractors. And I know that you permit the use of computers and cell phones when they're necessary for business..."

"But not trucks or any motor vehicles," the bishop cut him off. He sat upright and sighed heavily. "As for marrying Krystal, I have reservations about whether you'll truly fit in here, Jed."

Jed was astounded. "May I ask why?"

"I've heard rumors that you've already been driving

a bus. I didn't know whether to believe them until just now."

Jed's eyebrows shot up. "I won't lie. I test-drove the bus to assess whether I could handle it. It seemed pointless to ask for permission if I wasn't even capable of driving it."

"But that's precisely what concerns me," the bishop replied. "You should have sought permission first, then learned to drive the bus if approved. That's the process anyone else in this community would have followed."

Jed lowered his gaze. In the past, he'd always managed by bending the rules. It seemed that strategy wouldn't fly in this community.

"Have you nothing to say?" the bishop prodded.

"You're right," Jed admitted. "I apologize."

"And you nearly ran over one of our members with that bus. I was shocked when I heard that."

"From Matthew, I assume?"

The bishop remained silent for a moment before delivering his final verdict. "It grieves me to say this, but I believe for the safety of our community, it would be best if you went back to where you belong."

Jed's heart pounded at those words. What would this mean for him and Krystal?

It seemed Matthew had achieved his goal. Jed couldn't ask Krystal to abandon the quilt store she loved so much, and he wasn't confident that she would even consider it. Her independence was one of the qualities he admired about her.

He swallowed hard, considering revealing Matthew's recent actions, but decided against it. He didn't want to stoop that low. "Okay. Thanks for hearing me out. I'll leave by the end of the week."

With a heavy heart, Jed bid the bishop farewell and left the house. He had no idea how he'd break the news to Krystal. He couldn't bear to witness her disappointment when he told her their shared dream was over before it had begun. As he headed back to Samuel's buggy, the reality of having to leave this place he'd begun to consider home washed over him.

He'd been welcomed with open arms, like a member of the family.

And now he had to leave.

The hardest part was still to come—he had to tell Krystal.

CHAPTER 31

On Monday, Debbie was working away in her tea stall, going over the words she wanted to say to Fritz about Peter. As she prepared her special tea blend and carefully placed it into small bags, a voice interrupted her. "Hello, Debbie."

She looked up and smiled when she saw Fritz standing there. "Fritz!" She was delighted it was Fritz and not his brother. "This is a nice surprise. I thought you had things to do today."

"I do, but I missed you, so I thought I'd come by and say hello," he replied.

"It's so good to see you! I was hoping you'd come to the house later."

"How are you doing?" he asked.

Debbie knew it was now or never. She couldn't hold it inside of her anymore. "I'm okay. I really wanted to speak with you about something," she began, her voice dropping as she looked around them. The market was still, and there were not many people about, so Debbie continued, "It's concerning Peter." She paused briefly, biting her lip.

His brow furrowed with concern as he asked, "What is it?"

"I apologize for not telling you sooner. I didn't know how to say it."

He stood up straight and puffed out his chest. "What did he do?" Fritz asked.

"Well, he came to see me the other day," she said.

Fritz swallowed hard. "Why did he do that?"

"He demanded to know how I could marry you instead of him."

His mouth fell open. "What else did he say?"

Debbie could tell from the look on Fritz's face that he was not pleased with his brother's behavior. "That's pretty much all. Then he stormed off and said that neither of us would be seeing him again."

"But he left you for Maisy."

"I know. It didn't make sense to me either. I think he was upset with me. He said you and I hardly know each other, and in all the years that he and I were dating that…"

He put up his hand. "I get the idea. I'm so sorry, Debbie. Why didn't you tell me straight away?"

"I didn't want to upset you. I didn't want to ruin our time together. You go home in a couple of days."

Fritz was silent for a moment before responding. "I wondered why he left so soon."

Debbie looked at Fritz, trying to gauge his reaction.

He rubbed his chin for a few moments before looking back at her. "Debbie, I appreciate you telling me about this. I'm sorry that Peter put you in this position."

Debbie breathed a sigh of relief, grateful that Fritz wasn't mad at her. "Thank you for understanding. I just wanted to be honest with you."

"I'm glad you were. It's better to know the truth than to hide things from each other," Fritz said. "I'll deal with Peter when I get back home."

Debbie smiled at him, feeling a weight lifted off her shoulders. "Thank you, Fritz. I was worried about how you would react."

Fritz took her hand and gave it a gentle squeeze. "I'm not going to lie. I'm upset with my brother for what he said and did. But you're not to blame for any of it. You did the right thing by telling me."

Debbie suddenly wanted to throw her arms around him, but she held back. "I'm sorry I didn't tell you sooner."

Fritz shook his head. "There's no need to apologize. I'm just glad you did."

As they stood there, the market began to fill up with people again. "I should probably get back to work."

Fritz nodded. "Of course. I'll see you tomorrow. I can't see you tonight because my mother has guests for dinner and she wants me to be there. Or you could come too."

"Thanks, but I wouldn't want to leave Jared. I wouldn't bring him because he might not behave." Debbie hoped he'd insist she bring Jared along.

He nodded. "Okay. I'll be back here tomorrow."

"Come to dinner here tomorrow night," Debbie offered.

"I'd like that."

Debbie smiled. "I'll be looking forward to it."

As Fritz walked away, Debbie couldn't help but think about how lucky she was to have him in her life. She knew that dealing with Peter wouldn't be easy, but she also knew that she had Fritz by her side. She felt a sense of peace and security, knowing that Fritz would always be there for her no matter what. She'd chosen the right brother to marry.

The rest of the day went by in a blur as Debbie served customers and chatted with regulars.

CHAPTER 32

When the evening air was filled with the sounds of Krystal's returning horse and buggy, Jed was ready, waiting to help her unhitch the buggy. He'd spent Monday away from her quilt store, contemplating the best way to tell her that the bishop had suggested he leave.

The sight of Jed waiting for her sparked joy in Krystal, which soon turned to concern when she noticed the troubled expression on his face.

After caring for the horse, Jed took Krystal's hand, throwing an anxious glance at Matthew's tent on the porch.

"What's wrong?" she asked.

"I need you to stay away from Matthew. You're not safe around him."

Krystal turned to face Jed fully. "What do you mean?"

"I met with the bishop yesterday."

"You did?"

Jed nodded solemnly. "It didn't go well. Everything went awful in the most dreadful way."

Krystal's heart plummeted. "What happened?"

"Matthew told the bishop about the bus incident, implying that I was a negative influence on you and the community," Jed explained.

Krystal was upset. Her patience with Matthew had been exhausted. She began to stride toward the porch where Matthew was perched, but Jed grabbed her arm to hold her back.

"Wait a moment," he cautioned.

"But didn't you tell the bishop about Matthew's actions? He can't talk as though he's perfect. He's anything but perfect."

"No. I trust God will reveal everything."

Krystal held a different point of view. "God has also given you a voice, Jed," Krystal responded.

Jed smiled at her fiery spirit. "I considered saying something, but I'm not that kind of a person."

Krystal sighed. "I understand, but it's still infuriating."

"The worst thing is, the bishop looks at me a certain way now, and he didn't give us his blessing to marry."

Krystal suddenly realized how serious this was. "You asked him about that?"

"It came up in conversation."

Krystal suddenly knew how bad things had become. They should have thrown Matthew off the porch as soon as he arrived. "Take my hand." Krystal interlocked her fingers with Jed's, and together they climbed the porch steps.

Matthew watched them from inside his tent.

Once inside, they found everyone in the living room, and Krystal told everyone what had happened.

"I'm stunned," Debbie exclaimed.

"Jed, this is what happens when you don't obey the rules. I warned you about driving a vehicle," Ada scolded.

"I'm aware I made a mistake, but I wasn't trying to hurt anybody. It's my own fault. I took too many risks." Jed hung his head. "The bishop said I should go home, so I must leave."

Krystal gasped. "You didn't tell me that."

"I know. I'm sorry. I had hoped the bishop would be fine with it if I only drove the bus for the tours."

"You only had business on your mind. I understand," Krystal replied.

"Whether it was for work or not, it wasn't right. Are you happy to use the cart now?" Samuel asked.

Jed nodded. "More than happy if I'm allowed to stay."

"I'll talk with the bishop."

"Thank you, Samuel. I hope he changes his mind. There are so many reasons I want to stay here." Jed looked over at Krystal and smiled.

Samuel gave him a nod. "I'll do what I can."

"What will happen now?" Wilma asked.

"I don't think it's going to be good for him," Samuel added. "But I'll vouch for him. The bishop is a reasonable man."

Ada went over to the window, moved the curtains, and peeked outside. She saw Matthew sitting beside his tent, eating something out of a can. Suddenly she saw a buggy pull up. "Someone's here," she murmured.

Wilma came up behind her, and they both peered out the window together. The bishop got out of his buggy and walked toward the house.

"It's the bishop!" Ada whispered to everyone. Debbie and Krystal rushed to the window as well. They watched as the bishop called out to Matthew. Then the bishop walked up the porch stairs, and Matthew stood up.

CHAPTER 33

"*H*ello, Bishop Paul," Matthew said.

"I've come to speak with you, Matthew."

"With me?" Matthew was a little concerned about how the bishop knew he was there.

"That's right. It would be better to discuss this in private. Would you like to sit in my buggy?"

"Um... sure."

The bishop made his way back down the stairs, glancing at the windows. The curtains suddenly closed.

Matthew put down his can of food and followed the bishop to his buggy. Once he was sitting beside the bishop, he asked, "How did you know I was here?"

"People talk."

Matthew nodded, hoping the bishop wouldn't ask him to give up his quest and go home. Was that why the bishop had come? Matthew felt awful. He would have much rather had someone just ask him to go than to get the bishop involved.

"I hear you're spreading rumors," Bishop Paul said.

"No. I'd never do that."

"I just had an unusual visit from Andrew Weeks. He heard from your mouth that the girl he's courting can't have children."

Matthew shrugged his shoulders. "It's not a rumor. That's what she told me, or maybe I overheard it. I'm not sure, but I'm not lying."

"The young couple came to me upset. She was going to tell him, but your words were the ones to reach his ears. Not only that, your name has come up a lot lately."

Matthew hung his head. "My name?"

"I'm talking about you telling me about a visitor to this community driving a bus."

"He tried to kill me."

The bishop's eyebrows drew together. "I doubt that. And regarding Andrew Weeks and the young lady he's courting, it was something that should've stayed between them. It wasn't for you to share this information with anyone."

Matthew thought the whole thing had been blown out of proportion, but he could see the bishop had his mind made up. "Okay. I see that now. I'm sorry, but he shouldn't have been driving a bus, and I thought you should know."

"If that was the only time your name had come up,

that would've been different. It seems you have some ideas going on."

"What ideas?"

"Why were you on Wilma's porch?"

Matthew shrugged his shoulders. He didn't want to get into it with the bishop. "I just want Krystal back."

"That gives me an even clearer picture. It seems you've lashed out at two men this week. You should keep to yourself."

Matthew frowned, not understanding what the bishop was saying. "I haven't done anything wrong."

"Trouble can be caused by being a talebearer. I just want to caution you that—"

"I thought you'd want to know that someone in your community is driving a bus."

The bishop let out a deep sigh. "Matthew, it's not about whether you think what you're doing is wrong or not. It's about the consequences of your actions. You're spreading information that isn't yours to share and causing harm to others in the process. Consider the meaning behind what you were telling me. It wasn't the action. It was the meaning."

Matthew looked down, feeling guilty for causing trouble. "I didn't mean to hurt anyone," he uttered.

"Sometimes good intentions can lead to bad outcomes. You must be more careful about what you say to others and why you're saying it."

Matthew nodded, trying to take in the bishop's words. He knew he tended to blurt out things without thinking, but he never foresaw how much harm it could cause. "I didn't plan on saying that to Andrew. It just slipped out."

The bishop placed a hand on Matthew's shoulder. "I'm not here to scold you, Matthew. I'm here to help you learn and grow. We all make mistakes, but it's important that we learn from them and do better next time."

Matthew nodded again, feeling grateful for the bishop's kindness. "Thank you for talking to me, Bishop Paul. I'll try to be more careful in the future."

The bishop smiled. "I know you will, Matthew. And if you ever need someone to talk with or advice on handling a situation, you can always come to me."

With those words, the bishop said goodnight. Matthew got out of the buggy and returned to his tent to the sound of the bishop's horse clip-clopping away.

He picked up his half-eaten can of soup. Before he touched the spoon, he switched on his flashlight and saw his soup was overrun with ants.

He grunted. That's all he'd brought with him to eat.

Frustrated, Matthew threw the can across the porch, not caring where it landed. He was tired of living like this, hoping Krystal would see how much he cared.

She didn't care one bit. She preferred a careless man who didn't care about rules.

Matthew lay down on his makeshift bed, his mind racing with scattered thoughts. He couldn't get Krystal out of his head, no matter how hard he tried. He knew he had to do something to win her over and get everyone to like him again. But he wasn't sure what.

He couldn't just sit around waiting for Krystal to notice him. He had to do something to prove he was a man worth loving.

CHAPTER 34

*T*he following morning, Wilma took a stroll through the orchard with Red by her side.

Much to her surprise, the dog didn't bother her so much. It was evident that the dog had had some rough times, and so had she.

The dog also reminded her of Obadiah, but lately, everything reminded her of him.

It was almost as though she had a new purpose.

She sat beneath an apple tree and watched as Red rushed around without a care. At least now he didn't have to worry about where he'd get his next meal.

As Wilma daydreamed about Obadiah, she wondered where they would end up.

She remembered how often Obadiah looked at her with admiration in his eyes. Ada had noticed it too.

Suddenly Wilma noticed another dog sprinting

through the orchard and barreling toward Red. A man was following not far behind the dog.

As he came closer, Wilma saw it was Obadiah. He smiled from ear to ear as he approached and then sat down with her.

"I wasn't expecting you this morning," Wilma said.

"You weren't at the house, so I came looking for you."

"I'm glad you did."

"You are?" he asked.

"Yes."

The dogs began barking, and Wilma feared they were about to fight when Red took off in one direction, and Obadiah's dog chased it through the trees.

"They're only playing," Obadiah assured her.

"Good. They've each found a friend," Wilma said.

"So have I, I hope."

As Obadiah leaned closer and took her hand in his, nervousness fluttered in Wilma's stomach.

Wilma wanted to kiss him, but it was far too soon for anything like that.

Obadiah brushed his thumb over her knuckles as if reading her thoughts. "Is it wrong if I want to kiss you?" he whispered.

Wilma's heart skipped a beat. This was the moment she had yearned for since he'd come back into her life.

She threw caution and everything else to the wind and let go of everything she knew to be sensible. All sense left her head as she leaned into him. Their lips met in a sweet and tender kiss. The world around them faded away.

Distant sounds could be heard—dogs barking and birds chirping—but Wilma was in another world and another time.

When they parted, Obadiah looked at her with pure love in his eyes. "I've wanted to do that for so long," he said, his voice husky with emotion.

Wilma felt tears prick at the corners of her eyes. "Me too," she said, her voice barely above a whisper. They had an invisible connection, just like she'd had with Josiah, her first husband. That's how she knew this was real.

They sat together in silence. Wilma leaned her head on Obadiah's shoulder, feeling warm and content. She wanted to stay there forever, away from the worries of day-to-day life.

They didn't have to exchange words. It was as though Wilma knew his heart and his mind.

Eventually, though, he did speak. "I feel like I've been given a second chance, and I don't want to waste it."

Wilma's heart swelled with emotion. "I feel the same way, Obadiah. I don't want to waste this chance either, but..."

His eyebrows drew together. "But what?"

"I'm a little scared of what that means at our ages."

His lips curved upward. "Me too. I've never been married before."

"I've lost two husbands. It's a pain that I feel every day."

"I know how it must be for you, Wilma. And I understand if you're scared. We can take things slow. I want to make you happy."

Wilma's heart swelled with love for Obadiah. She knew she wanted to take a chance on him, to see where this newfound love could take them. "Okay," she softly agreed.

Red and Obadiah's dog returned, nipping at each other's heels. Wilma and Obadiah smiled at each other, feeling content and happy in each other's presence.

"I have to go back to Eli's house," Obadiah said regretfully. "But I don't want to leave you."

Wilma smiled. "Come back for dinner tonight. Bring Eli too."

"He'd love that, and so would I."

They stood up and walked back to the house, side by side.

When they got close to the house, Wilma knew she needed to learn more about him. She was too old to make any mistakes. Too many people depended on her.

"Obadiah, I need to ask you something," Wilma said.

"Yes, go ahead."

"Why did you come back here?"

"Let's sit on the porch. I feel you've got a few more questions for me."

"Just one or two." Once they were seated, Wilma began, "You mentioned that you recently had a relationship with someone."

He nodded. "It didn't go too well."

The last thing Wilma wanted was to have trouble with another woman if she was still in love with him. "I understand it's over between the two of you, but does she also want it to be over?"

Obadiah rolled up his sleeve, displaying the large scar on his arm. "When I attempted to leave her, she became angry and scalded me with hot water."

Wilma gasped in surprise. "You can't be serious."

"She has quite an explosive temperament."

Now Wilma was worried. "What would cause a woman to do that?"

Obadiah moved his sleeve back down. "She wanted marriage, and I wasn't ready. Things got heated. From her side, not mine."

Wilma could feel her heart aching for him. "I'm so sorry that happened to you, Obadiah. No one should have to go through that kind of pain, physical or emotional."

"It's been a difficult time for me. But it's made me realize what I want in life and, more importantly, who I want it with."

Wilma looked at him, her eyes searching his face for

any sign of doubt or hesitation. She found none. "And who is that?"

"It's you, Wilma. You made an impression on me years ago."

Wilma's heart skipped a beat.

They were interrupted by Ada and Samuel arriving.

"Can we keep this between ourselves for now?" Wilma asked. "I need to get used to it before we start telling others how we feel."

"Sure, whatever suits you."

They both stood up. Wilma was not going to tell Ada about the kiss they shared. She'd keep that to herself for now.

She could hear Ada's voice in her head, lecturing her that they really didn't know that much about him.

LATER THAT EVENING, Debbie arrived home early, and Jared was outside with Samuel while Ada and Wilma discussed Debbie's wedding.

She couldn't stop thinking about the things that Peter had said the other day. She'd tried to push them from her mind, but the awful words kept haunting her.

The emotions bubbled up inside her, and she burst into tears, wiping them away, but not before Wilma noticed.

"What's wrong?" Wilma asked.

Ada came rushing to her side, leaving the shelling of the peas, and sat next to her. "What's the matter?"

"Peter came to see me at my stall the other day," she began.

Ada frowned. "Why?"

"What did he want?" Wilma asked.

"Fritz was under the impression that he was doing well and had grown a lot since... what happened. He said Peter was pleased about us getting married."

"And?" Ada asked, her eyes bugging out.

"He didn't seem pleased. He seemed the opposite. He started saying things like Fritz was a bachelor and he wouldn't go through with the wedding." Tears trickled down Debbie's cheeks.

"No." Wilma shook her head. "Don't listen to that. He was the one who asked you to marry him, *jah?*"

Debbie sniffed. "Peter has left and gone back home. I told Fritz. He seemed okay, but will he blame me?"

"No. Of course not. Don't give it another thought. Is Fritz coming for the evening meal tonight?"

"Yes, but he's only here for a few days and hasn't seen me that much. I can't even remember half of what Peter said, but it wasn't nice."

Ada put her arm around Debbie. "Ignore the whole thing."

Debbie wiped her eyes. "I don't know. We've ignored Matthew, but he's still living on the porch."

Ada looked helplessly over at Wilma.

"It might be time to put a stop to Matthew doing

that. Now, don't worry about anything, Debbie. Fritz loves you, and he should know his brother better than anyone," Wilma said.

"How does that help me?" Debbie sniffed again.

"What Wilma means is that he'll stand by you. It sounds like Peter might be jealous. You didn't want to marry him. You hesitated for so long."

Debbie wiped away a tear. "I know, but it's so awkward that they're brothers. It's not ideal. Not ideal at all. Then I think, why is my life always so messed up?"

"It's not."

"I'm not talking to my parents or Jared's grandparents. They're out of my life. I want to be close with Fritz's family, but that's not getting off to a good start."

Wilma put her arm around her. "It's not all bad. We all love you, and that's no secret."

"Wilma's right. You've got Jared and us, and you'll soon be married to a *wunderbaar* man. Wilma and I had our doubts about him, but we think he's all right now, don't we, Wilma?"

"Oh yes. Now go and wash your face so you'll look good when he arrives. We've also got Obadiah and Eli joining us tonight."

With a slight nod of agreement, Debbie forced herself up from the table and walked to the bathroom. The cool water against her flushed skin helped to calm her. Staring into her small hand mirror, she looked at her red-rimmed eyes and tried to see the woman Fritz loved, the woman Wilma and Ada had faith in.

Shaking her head, she allowed herself a small, wistful smile. Despite the chaos, her life was not a tragedy; it was a tapestry woven with complex threads, embroidered with mistakes, memories, and moments of pure joy. She didn't regret a single stitch; it had made her into the woman she was. The woman Fritz wanted to marry.

Drying her face, she returned to the kitchen, feeling a surge of determination. She couldn't control Peter or Matthew, but she could choose to focus on the love she had for Fritz.

"You're right, both of you," Debbie announced as she re-entered the kitchen. The determination in her voice surprised even her. "I am loved. We are loved. And we don't need to care about what Peter or anyone else says."

Ada and Wilma looked at her with matching expressions of surprise. The room was filled with a new kind of energy, one that was palpable and empowering. A silent agreement passed between them. From that moment, they decided to stand strong against anyone who tried to unravel their happiness.

As if on cue, the front door creaked open, and the cheerful sound of laughter filled the house. The tension dissolved further as Jared burst into the kitchen with Samuel behind him. Fritz followed, looking as ruggedly handsome as ever. Five minutes later, Obadiah and Eli arrived.

As they sat down to eat, Debbie knew she was exactly where she was meant to be. The past was behind her, and she had so much happiness in front of her.

Jed also had good news for everyone. Samuel had seen the bishop on Jed's behalf, and the bishop told him he'd already decided to allow Jed to stay.

CHAPTER 35

*O*nce they had finished dinner, Krystal and Jed quietly stepped out the back door, avoiding the company of Matthew, who still lingered on the porch.

"I'm sorry Matthew is constantly around the house. It makes it hard to have a private conversation," Krystal said.

"I understand. I do my best to ignore him. It's tougher on you, seeing he hardly leaves you alone."

They settled down on the back steps, and Jed, his throat feeling dry, bravely broached a subject that had been on his mind. "I've developed deep feelings for you. Are you experiencing the same?"

She responded, "You know how I feel. You are perfectly right for me. We'll have a good life together, I know it."

A wide grin spread across Jed's face. "Krystal, would you agree to be my wife? We've mentioned this before, but I've never formally proposed, have I?"

Krystal chuckled. "You haven't. So you're asking me now?"

"I am, officially. And don't argue that it's too soon. Too soon for who? Not me."

"I wasn't going to say it's too soon. I couldn't imagine being married to anyone but you."

"Truly? So what's your answer? I have to hear you say it."

"Yes."

He gently grasped her hand and squeezed it.

"I can provide for us until your tour business is up and running," Krystal said.

"I have a lot to sort out, but I've never been more enthusiastic about anything. Before meeting you, I questioned whether I would ever get married."

Krystal nodded. "I had the same thoughts. It seemed like the local men ignored me because I wasn't born Amish."

"I recall you mentioning that earlier, but I find it unbelievable. While I was born into this lifestyle, that doesn't mean I never question it. Of course, some of our rules feel unnecessary, but I still plan to stay. You chose this lifestyle willingly. I believe that makes you stronger."

She was touched to hear his viewpoint. "I share that

belief. I can't understand why others don't see things in the same way."

"I suspect it might be because they believe our life-style would be too demanding, and you'd start longing for your old life – the freedom to watch movies, do as you please, and wear whatever you want."

"I hadn't considered that. Maybe that's what they believe, but I follow through once I commit to something or someone."

They sat there for a while longer, talking about their future together and dreaming of what was to come.

They were then interrupted by Ada, who opened the back door. "Oh, here you are. We're going home soon, Jed."

"Okay. Thanks, Ada. I'll be there in a minute."

When Ada closed the door, they both stood up. "I guess I'll see you tomorrow," Jed said.

They hugged each other before they made their way inside.

ALL NIGHT WILMA had been on edge. She could feel Obadiah looking at her throughout the whole meal. All she could do was avoid his gaze. The last thing she wanted was for Ada to guess there was something more between them than she'd let on.

Ada would only lecture her, and she didn't want that.

Thankfully, Obadiah and Eli left without Obadiah trying to have a private moment with her. If that had happened, Ada would've asked questions until she got answers.

CHAPTER 36

*T*he next day, Malachi came home, excitement buzzing in his voice. "Zeke asked me to deliver a message to Harriet and Melvin."

"About what?" Cherish asked.

"Seems there is a house that's vacant and ready to be leased."

"That's great news. Why can't Zeke tell them?"

Malachi shrugged. "Not sure. He might be too scared he'll be stuck over there talking."

"That's true. Harriet does talk a lot. So tell me about the house."

"The owner had to dash off somewhere. I don't know much more than that, but Zeke told me where I can find the key. They can look at it today."

"That's great news!" Cherish knew Favor would be delighted.

Pushing his hat back, Malachi grinned. "I'm guessing Harriet'll find somethin' wrong with it, no matter how spot-on it might be."

Cherish laughed softly. "Oh, don't be so sure. She might love it."

"Well, we better trot over and tell them. It's just a hop and a skip away from Simon and Favor's place."

"You're right. They'll love being that close." Cherish stepped to one side, trying to hide the shopping bags she'd been sorting through.

Too late.

Malachi glanced at all her purchases. "What's all this?"

His eyes popped wide as Cherish pulled out baby clothes from one bag. "You're having a baby?" He rushed to Cherish, swinging her into his arms.

Cherish let out a laugh, "No! Stop it."

Frowning, Malachi put her down.

"It's Favor who's pregnant, not me. We're sworn to secrecy for now. She hasn't even told *Mamm* or Simon's folks."

"So you went shopping for her then?"

"That's right. More's on the way."

"More babies?"

"No, silly. More things. We're giving them a crib and a dresser for the baby's clothes." Noticing his surprise, she quickly added, "We've got enough money. What's the use of it just sitting in the bank?"

"You never know what's round the next corner. We might need the money."

"Simon and Favor moved here to be close to us. Simon has no work right now, and they have a baby on the way. Can you imagine how stressed they must be?"

"I get you. You're right. But remember, we already gave them a hand with the house and the land."

Cherish crossed her arms. "We didn't give it to them. They had to pay for it."

"Not much, though."

"Anyway, that's how you wanted to help them, not me! Isn't the money ours to use?"

With a sigh, Malachi replied, "I'm glad to lend a hand, just don't go overboard. If we end up with nothing, we won't be able to help anyone else."

"I get it."

Rubbing his neck, he said, "I hope you do."

Once they arrived at Favor's house, they knocked on the door.

"Harriet, Melvin, we got some good news," Malachi announced as they were invited in.

Harriet and Melvin sat on the sofa, their eyes widening at the mention of good news. Harriet spoke first, "What is it?"

Malachi grinned. "Zeke told you about a house, right?"

"Not directly. He told Simon about one, though." Harriet nodded.

"The owners have left and the house is empty. They're leasing it now. They've left the key under the mat."

Melvin looked hesitant. "What's wrong with it?"

Cherish stifled a laugh.

"Nothing. I'm told it's perfectly fine."

Harriet and Melvin shared a look before Harriet spoke up, "Can we go see it?"

"Of course," Malachi said, his excitement growing. "We can go there now."

Harriet and Melvin both nodded, eager to see the potential new home.

"I'll come too," Simon said. "I'll just tell Favor where I'm going."

Harriet and Melvin took in its old-fashioned charm as they approached the empty house. It had a spacious yard with a picket fence and a cozy front porch. They could already imagine themselves sitting out there in the mornings, sipping coffee and watching the world go by.

The inside of the house was just as told, nice, with high ceilings and old-fashioned details that made it feel like home. Harriet was immediately drawn to the large kitchen, where she could picture herself cooking meals.

As they explored the rest of the house, they couldn't help but fall in love with it. They turned to Malachi and Cherish, beaming with excitement.

"We love it," Harriet said, her eyes shining.

Melvin nodded in agreement. "It's perfect."

Malachi grinned. "I'm glad you both like it. What do you think, Simon?"

"I agree. What do we need to do to make it official?" Melvin asked.

CHAPTER 37

A few days later, Favor was well enough to get out of bed and get dressed. She hoped the dreadful morning sickness was behind her.

Upon entering the kitchen, she found herself frozen in place, her eyes tracing the novel design along the walls. "Who did this in here?" she called out.

Simon, overhearing her from the living room, rushed in. "Ma did it," he confessed, looking apologetic. He then lowered his voice to a whisper, "We can paint over it. I didn't know she planned to do this. I was working outside when it happened, and by the time I returned, she'd done this."

Favor pressed her fingers to his lips, silencing his apologies. "I love it!" she declared, her eyes sparkling at the sight of the vibrant flowers that now brightened their kitchen.

Simon exhaled a sigh of relief. "Are you certain?"

"Yes."

His shoulders lowered. "Good. Ma and Pa have some news for you."

Favor's grin widened. "About moving out?" she whispered back.

"Yes." Holding her hand, he guided her to the living room, where Harriet made room for her on the couch.

"What's happening?" Favor inquired.

Melvin took over the conversation. "We're transitioning to our new place tomorrow."

Favor was taken aback, a ripple of sudden anxiety coursing through her. Who would take care of her? "Are you sure the house is suitable?"

"We love it, right, Melvin?"

"It'll serve us well until we find a place to purchase. We'll discuss buying the last block with the bishop. If that works out, we'll be neighbors."

Favor could feel Simon's gaze on her. She knew he was curious about her lack of excitement. "I'm glad that you've found a place."

"We'll need to transport our belongings from our old house, Melvin. It seems like this town is where we'll settle for good." Harriet's grin was contagious.

Favor reciprocated the smile, genuinely pleased for her in-laws. "I'm certain you'll find happiness here."

"We already are happy." Harriet tenderly patted Favor's hand. "And we're incredibly grateful for you and Simon providing us shelter during our search."

Favor shrugged. "We were happy to help."

Melvin said, "We can't thank you enough for your kindness."

Rising to her feet, Favor added, "Oh, Harriet, the kitchen looks absolutely beautiful, thanks to your touch."

Harriet gifted her with a warm smile. "I'm pleased you appreciate it."

"I think I might rest," Favor said, weariness slipping into her voice.

"Do you need anything before I leave?" Harriet asked, appearing as concerned as ever.

"No, I'm good. Later, I'll get up and prepare the evening meal. Tonight, you should take a break, Harriet. You've been handling everything recently."

"But I've already cooked dinner. It just needs warming up when it's time."

"Thank you. I'll make up for everything when I'm better." As Favor made her way to her bedroom, an unfamiliar pang tugged at her heartstrings. In their unique, often challenging ways, her in-laws had intertwined with her and Simon's day-to-day life. Yet she also understood that this transition was essential. They needed their own space, particularly with the imminent arrival of their first child.

In bed, she closed her eyes, inhaling deeply in an attempt to quell her churning nerves. A child was fast approaching, and she'd never shouldered such an immense responsibility. Reopening her eyes, she saw Simon framed in the doorway.

"Hey," he murmured softly.

"Hey," she echoed back.

"Are you doing okay?"

Favor released a shaky sigh. "I don't know. I feel a bit scared about everything. The baby coming, and all. I've never done this before."

"It's perfectly normal to be nervous. We'll do this together."

A small smile twitched at Favor's lips. "I know. I just wish I could switch off the worrying."

Simon crossed the room, settling down beside her. "You'll learn to. It may take time, but you'll find your way."

Favor nestled her head into his shoulder. "I hope so. It's going to be strange with your parents gone."

"Yes, but it'll be a good kind of strange. It'll be just us, as we always planned." Simon's lips brushed her forehead, planting a gentle kiss. "And our little bundle of joy," he added.

Favor placed a hand on her belly. It was flat and she couldn't wait for it to grow. "Yes, our bundle of joy," she echoed softly. "I hope we'll be good parents."

"I have no doubt. We might stumble along the way, but we'll give our best. And we'll always have each other for support."

Favor felt a sliver of reassurance seep into her. "I just don't want to fail."

"We'll probably make some mistakes, I'm sure of it. But we'll get through it."

Favor lifted her gaze to meet Simon's, a rush of love flooding her. "You're right," she affirmed. "We'll figure this all out together."

Simon's smile mirrored her own. "Together," he said.

CHAPTER 38

Favor's sleepless night had left her in a state of turmoil, her mind consumed with anxious thoughts. She lay in bed, her body exhausted and her appetite nonexistent.

As she listened to the sounds of activity outside her window, Favor's unsteady steps guided her to the window. The sight of organized chaos unfolded before her eyes as Simon assisted Harriet and Melvin in packing their few belongings into the buggy, preparing for their departure.

A peculiar sensation stirred within Favor, a realization that washed over her like the rolling waves of an unexpected tide. Despite Harriet's nagging and overbearing nature, she couldn't help but wonder if she could face pregnancy without her mother-in-law's presence.

Slumping back into the comforting embrace of her bed, Favor's mind raced with conflicting thoughts. She couldn't deny the countless instances where Harriet's help over the last few days had been invaluable. Her consistent support, in her own unique way, had eased Favor's worries a little and brought a sense of stability.

A gentle knock on the doorframe drew Favor's attention away from her swirling thoughts. Looking up, she saw Harriet, her face glowing with maternal concern. "We're setting off now, dear."

"So soon?" Favor's voice barely hid her disappointment, fear creeping into her words.

Harriet's lips curved into a warm smile, her eyes filled with understanding. "Yes, it's time for us to go."

Favor's heart sank, the weight of her worries pressing upon her. She hesitated for a moment before mustering the courage to speak. "Ma, I... I want you to know how much your support has meant to me. You've been here for me in so many ways, and I'm grateful for everything you've done."

Harriet's expression softened, her eyes shimmering with appreciation. "Oh, my dear, it warms my heart to hear you say that. It's been my pleasure to help."

Favor nodded, hoping she'd be able to cope.

As Harriet moved closer, embracing Favor, a sense of togetherness enveloped them. The room filled with the warmth of their shared connection.

"I'll miss you," Favor said.

"I'll be back every day."

"You will?"

"Yes. I'll stay each day until you're better."

"Thank you. Please be here early tomorrow," Favor asked.

"Alright," Harriet murmured, her voice barely louder than a whisper. "If that's what you want."

"Yes."

In that moment, all the annoyances, the frequent quarrels, and the moments of exasperation faded away. In their place was a simple request—an olive branch extended toward a more harmonious future.

Harriet beamed, her heart swelling with a mix of surprise and happiness. "Bye for now," Harriet whispered as she left the room. Her steps were lighter than they had been in a long time.

As Harriet walked outside, the world seemed a little brighter. The sight of the packed buggy greeted her, and she knew they wouldn't be in their new house for long. She was certain that the bishop would allow them to buy the land next to Simon.

Meanwhile, Favor sighed with relief and gratitude, allowing her tired eyes to flutter closed. The weight that had been on her shoulders seemed to lighten considerably. She allowed herself to drift into a peaceful sleep, knowing that the coming days would bring a new chapter for all of them. And she looked forward to it with a heart full of hope.

≈

WILMA LOOKED out her kitchen window and saw Obadiah. It was perfect timing because she was alone since Ada was at her own home doing what she called 'much-needed house cleaning.'

Wilma went out to meet him.

"Hey, Wilma," he said, a hint of nervousness in his voice. "I was wondering if you would like to go for a walk with me."

Wilma's heart fluttered at the invitation. "I would love to," she replied, trying to keep her voice steady. She hadn't been able to stop thinking of the secret kiss they'd shared—something that she'd managed to keep from Ada.

They set off on a path that led through the rows of apple trees, the sunlight casting dappled light across their faces. Red appeared behind them, but he kept a distance as though he sensed they'd rather be alone.

They walked in comfortable silence for a while until Obadiah spoke up. "I know we've talked a little about our future, and I still want that, but I need to go home for a while."

Now Wilma knew how Debbie felt with Fritz living far away. She didn't want to go through all the ups and downs of wondering when he'd come back—if he'd come back at all.

Obadiah looked at her with fierce determination in

his eyes. "I love you, Wilma." His voice was raw with emotion.

Wilma swallowed hard. "I have strong feelings for you too." Wilma looked down. "But I can't see that this will work."

He stared at her open-mouthed. "Why not?"

She took a deep breath, preparing to reveal her innermost feelings. "I have been through so much loss. I can't risk going through those emotions again."

"I understand that, but think about the happiness we could bring one another. Maybe you should be having different thoughts," he suggested.

"My life is consistent now. Each day is the same. That's the way I'm used to it going."

He tipped his hat back on his head. "You want to live the same day over and over?"

"Yes."

He turned away from her for a moment. Wilma couldn't tell what he was thinking.

Finally, he turned back. "I understand," he said, his voice soft. "But I still love you, Wilma. And if you ever change your mind, I'll be waiting."

Wilma nodded. She loved him too, but she had to protect her heart. Grief was the worst thing in the world, a feeling that no one understood unless they'd been through it.

They hugged each other tightly, taking comfort in each other's embrace. For a few moments, nothing else in the world mattered. They were just two people holding onto each other and hoping for the best.

Eventually, they pulled away from each other. Obadiah gave her one last look before he walked away.

No words were said. No words were needed.

Wilma watched him go.

It had been thrilling to feel the spark of love again, but seeing it end so soon was bittersweet. She was certain she had made the right decision but couldn't help feeling a pang of sadness as she watched him disappear into the distance.

As she closed her eyes, memories flashed through her mind—memories of the children she had raised, their laughter, their tears, their triumphs, and their failures. It had been a hard life, but it had been a good one too.

Wilma opened her eyes and looked up at the sky. The sun cast an orange glow across the trees. She took a deep breath and let the cool breeze wash over her face. For the first time in ages, she felt at peace.

She took a deep breath in and then strolled back to her house. She might not have a husband, but she had good friends and family. Each one of them had their flaws and funny ways. Ada was opinionated, and everything had to go her way. Jared was a constant handful, and so was Matthew. Jed drove a bus, and Iris had been allowed to name her baby brother.

"Never a dull moment," Wilma muttered as she pushed open the back door.

She looked back and saw Red still over near the apple trees. "Come on, Red. Dinner time."

Red came bounding toward her.

Thank you for reading Her Amish Wish.

THE NEXT BOOK IN THE SERIES.

Book 38
Amish Harvest Time

As the orchard overflows with ripe fruit, Ada's creative spark ignites an extraordinary idea: an apple pie contest to unite the community and support a worthy cause. Amidst the rolling dough flurry and warm spices aroma, a surprise visitor arrives, setting female hearts aflutter.

As secrets unravel and new connections form, this captivating family saga explores love, faith, and the enduring bonds that hold a family together.

If you're looking for these books in audiobook, paperback, or large print, you can shop directly from Samantha at:

SamanthaPriceAuthor.com

ABOUT SAMANTHA PRICE

Samantha Price is a USA Today bestselling and Kindle All Stars author of Amish romance books and cozy mysteries. She was raised Brethren and has a deep affinity for the Amish way of life, which she has explored extensively with over a decade of research.

She is mother to two pampered rescue cats, and a very spoiled staffy with separation issues.

SamanthaPriceAuthor.com

THE AMISH BONNET SISTERS

Book 25 A Season for Change

Book 26 Amish Farm Mayhem

Book 27 The Stolen Amish Wedding

Book 28 A Season for Second Chances

Book 29 A Change of Heart

Book 30 The Last Wedding

Book 31 Starting Over

Book 32 Love and Cherish

Book 33 Amish Neighbors

Book 34 Her Amish Quilt

Book 35 A Home of Their Own

Book 36 A Chance for Love

Book 37 Her Amish Wish

ALL SAMANTHA PRICE BOOK SERIES

Amish Maids Trilogy

Amish Love Blooms

Amish Misfits

The Amish Bonnet Sisters

Amish Women of Pleasant Valley

Ettie Smith Amish Mysteries

Amish Secret Widows' Society

Expectant Amish Widows

Seven Amish Bachelors

Amish Foster Girls

Amish Brides

Amish Romance Secrets

Amish Christmas Books

Amish Wedding Season

Made in the USA
Monee, IL
03 August 2023

40408205R00142